Whispers on the Trampoline

Sarah Radford

Whispers on the Trampoline

To Anna, Stephanie, Michaela, John and Sophie
my five most precious inspirations

Whispers on the Trampoline
ISBN 978 1 76041 106 0
Copyright © Sarah Radford 2016
Cover photo: Kaille Kerr

First published 2016 by
GINNINDERRA PRESS
PO Box 3461 Port Adelaide 5015
www.ginninderrapress.com.au

You Are Invited to 'Whispers on the Trampoline'

Where: The Big House

When: This Twelfth Night, 9 p.m.

Why: To Remember

What to bring: Your self, your whole self and nothing but yourself

14 January 2011

To: Katie, Jack

<u>Subject: Surprise</u>

Hello All,

Take a look at this. It was amongst the stuff Pa left when he moved out. Look at the writing. Of course, you recognise the writing. That's from her diaries. Our Mama's diaries.

Lots of love and happy reading

Bella

<u>Attachment:</u>

Diary: May Day 1982!

Bargain! Took Bella out in the pram for a walk today and down Eliza Street, and there – just sitting all alone on the footpath, was a chest of drawers with a sign 'FREE' on it. It was a hideous '70s mission brown paint, but it was walnut underneath. I could see it when I took one of the drawers out to look inside. Who would paint over walnut? Papa will help me with the finish after I've stripped it. I can't wait to get my hands on it! It's bizarre, I have this buzz in my spine and my hands are itching. It feels just the same when I'm about to play a piece of music for the first time: the key, the timing, the unique yet familiar blending of notes dance around in my head and spill onto the piano keys out of my fingers. Magic.

My students this afternoon were Daisy and Ruby Milne, who had a distracted lesson, but they were happy enough with their chocolate chip cookies afterwards. I think Daisy could actually do something with her piano if she practised. She has a real 'touch' already, and she occasionally strokes the keys as if they were some treasure. I hope she keeps playing.

So I had to wait aaaaall day for Steve, and I was so worried that someone else might have picked the drawers up before he got home. It felt like weeks before he finally walked in. He was actually quite unimpressed with the idea at first. And he's an engineer! Aren't they supposed to be creative in a weird, technical, structural kind of way? Poor Steve hadn't even really got through the door before I pounced on him. He was quite interested for a minute – that was before he heard what it was exactly I was trying to involve him in. He was disappointed when he heard my actual proposition – not what he was hoping for at all – but he is an indulgent man. I must remember to thank him appropriately…

He naturally wanted to wait until after tea, but there's no time like the present, right? I packed Bella into the pram while Steve pulled out the sack truck and some ropes. I had to wrap Bella up snugly in a blanket to protect her sore ears. Third infection this year, poor bundle. We girls challenged Daddy to a race for the end of the street and he most obligingly lost, much to Bella's delight.

And there it was. Yes, waiting for me, all alone in the fading light. Steve managed to load it onto the sack truck and tie the ropes around the drawers with one of his clever knots so they didn't slide out. I nearly skipped all the way home. Fortunately for everyone else, we all needed to eat when we got back, so there was no time to begin work on it, or I'd probably be out there still. It's ridiculous; it's like waiting for Christmas morning.

Tonight's not looking easy. Bella is cutting her molars. Each tooth is a torture, poor kid. Each and every single tooth. I am pouting above her little head, because I won't be able to start on the drawers tonight. Sigh. Well, I will just cuddle my little bundle and explain to her the entire, wonderful process of stripping, sanding and varnishing wood. I'm sure she has some useful comments to make in between this very sad song she's singing me.

15 January 2011

To: Bella, Jack

<u>Subject: I love it! And…I have news for you!</u>

Thank you! Thank you! This is so cool. Are you going to scan any more? It was like listening to her voice. So my news – WE ARE HAVING A BABY! First ultrasound coming up.

Katie xoxo

PS: baby's the size of a walnut

19 January 2011

To: Bella, Katie

<u>Re: I love it!</u>

So, Uncle Jack here. I'll be a very useful resource for your child, Katie. Just ask Bella's two. I don't have a lot of time to read, Bella, so don't expect a lot of feedback, but I'm sure Katie will fill in the gaps.

J.

PS: She talks like Katie.

21 January 2011

To: Katie, Jack

<u>Subject: invitation for dinner at the bachelor pad</u>

Glad you both got it and Jack, I know you don't have a lot of time in your career for reading. It's not compulsory, but these are our mother's diaries. Just file it somewhere. It's now yours.

Katie, it was so good to speak to you about your baby. This is the new generation of cousins now. My two are really excited. But not as excited as you sound about the diaries. When you get back from holidays, you can read them as well.

As you know, we helped our dear old dad to move into his new house last weekend. Pa looks sort of settled and comfortable. BTW, everyone is invited to dinner next Friday night at his new bachelor pad. He's cooking. It's going to be weird for Lachie and me having the whole of the Big House to ourselves after all these years. It's a bit like starting out on our own for the first time, even though we've been married for seven years and have two kids. You guys had better keep coming around and filling it up again – often.

As we were packing the last trailer load, Pa told me he'd left a few things under the house. You know, where he kept all his work records and stuff. He told me he had everything he wanted and that I could decide what needed to be passed around to everyone. It was Mama's 'Memory Makers' box…

Some boxes of our drawings and schoolbooks, one for each of us; and an old brown globite suitcase. It weighed a tonne. She had a whole stack of them. Do you remember how she used to pile them up in corners as if someone was about to go on an exciting holiday somewhere in the world? Pa told us to go through it all later and that he already had what he wanted from them.

I was too tired last night to do more than just glance at it, but this morning I went down. It was like walking through Aladdin's cave.

Jack, Katie and I thought we would go through most of it together sometime; what do you think? I found Mama's diary – as you saw – and I'll give you both a copy. I'm flooded with memories, so you guys get to listen to me – for once – at great length:

Once, the three of us lay on our backs on the trampoline and looked up at the stars. I wonder if you guys remember it. The stars were brilliant because the moon was small, just a fingernail sliver in the sky. It was not long after Mama died and we needed new traditions. We were still only children, still bereft by the loss of a mother, but intensely relieved she was no longer suffering. The only place to be was here. Here where we always went when there were secrets to be shared, problems to solve, decisions to be made or parents to avoid. We needed to feel the forward motion of the wheels again.

Without really understanding why, we all just climbed onto the trampoline together with the new puppy. Mica wiggled her body between us, anxious to be part of our little circle, licking our faces and chewing Jack's shoelaces. One of you – I think it was Katie – asked if we thought Mama could still see us and if she missed us at all, and would we remember her when we got to be there too.

So I replied how, when we went on camps or sleepovers, she would say that if we should feel the tiniest bit lonely, or very lonely, or even just curious, then we should look up to the stars and the moon and know that somewhere the same light would be shining on her too and she would be thinking of us and loving us; the moonlight would be her kiss goodnight, and sleep would be her cuddle. Well, I think it's the same thing, only maybe now she's part of that light.

Then, Jack, you whispered in a hushed voice that you were scared you might not recognise her when you got there too. I said I knew you would because there's a special sort of knowing between family. Pa calls them soul ties. They're special and unbreakable when they're good and in the right place.

We have a story together, one that begins 'Once upon a time' and finishes with 'and they all lived all the days of their lives.'

Anyway, we three eventually just lay there and held hands and Mica quietly thumped her black tail against Jack's legs with her nose tucked under his feet. It was good to lie there and look at the stars. The warm late summer airbrushed across our faces and we could hear Pa finish off the dishes on the other side of the big windows where she used to stand, behind the closed doors of our house. This was our time, now and present. We would always be three different facets of the same stone.

'I remember,' I began, 'the sound of her voice as she sang in the kitchen. She had a terrible voice, but it was hers. We laughed because it was true. She could never hold a key and often made up the words because she couldn't remember the right ones. Even to nursery rhymes. This was really funny, because she was so gifted at music. I bet the great musical masters rolled over in their graves every time she hummed their masterpieces.'

'I remember the look on her face when we made her surprises,' Katie added.

'Oh, yes!' I went on. 'Do you remember, Jack, when you wanted to make pancakes for her breakfast and then tried to clean up the floor like Pippi Longstocking? Didn't we laugh?' Do you remember that?

Jack, you just nodded, but wouldn't say anything, but when we began laughing, you joined in. We laughed so much that Mica had to get up and rearrange herself away from us. We just lay there until the mosquitoes drove us inside and Pa kissed us all goodnight.

Reading her diaries, I can see how this could be another chance for us to pull out memories again, turn them over, laugh, cry, spit – whatever :) and finally put them back in their proper place. We weren't too good at saying goodbye back then, but here's a second chance. Poor Pa, I wonder what his diary would say. Anyway, I'll send more later.

Love as always

Bella

PS: Who's coming to dinner next Friday? Be sure to tell Pa.

2 February 2011

To: Katie, Jack

<u>Subject: More threads and more thoughts</u>

Hi again,

Reading through her early stuff as I scan is like an unravelling backwards, like threads that have come loose. I have more thoughts – I hope you guys don't mind. Feel free to join in. In fact, please join in. It'll do us all good.

One by one, we appeared until there were the five of us. That's how it was. No less and no more. Just five. There will always be the five of us somehow, because even when a person's no longer there, they're still with us. There's always a hole shaped the way they fitted into our life, because once upon a time we shared space together. And that is how it is. I don't know why, it just is. We had everything and very little to begin with, but we always had us.

Our story began in a humble home as all good stories do. Humble homes can be ordinary places filled with extraordinary people. Living is what turns ordinary events into extraordinary adventures. That's the magic that people we love speak over our lives. And she loved us. Pa told us he was the richest king in the world because he had us, and Mama agreed. I don't know that it was the best idea for us to have, because no one else believed us when we had holes in our shoes, or couldn't afford new pencils. But it was a lovely thought, wasn't it? Anyway, that changed for you, Jack. Once she found out she could turn more than random notes into sonatas. She began changing bits of wood into brand-new furniture, beautiful and unique. She had magic in her hands.

I don't know when the stories began, but she eventually wrote them down here in her diaries. But you'll see that. We loved the storytelling. I do remember her telling people it was part of standard 'crowd control' techniques, but I never saw anyone else use it. She told them at bedtime, she told them at mealtimes, she told them in the car.

She even told them to the cousins. What I realise now is why. They weren't crowd control techniques at all, they were memory makers. She was trying to teach us about our family and what she wanted our family to be, and who she wanted us to be, and what she would like to have given us: a castle, everything our hearts desired, and to live Happily Ever After. I don't know if she realised it at first, but I'm very certain she used the storytelling in the end. For the end.

There's a photo on Oma's shelf of all of us buried in the fallen wisteria, claret ash and maple leaves at their old house. Quite a few photos, really, as one by one, the numbers in the wheelbarrows increased.

Opa always waited until he couldn't wait any more before raking the leaves up. They fell and fell in great piles and mounds on to his paving, and then we would come around and heap them into the wheelbarrow. Mama would put us on top of the wheelbarrow and push us to be dumped with the leaves up the back of his garden. We would take it in turns to be the King of the Castle while she was gone. When I got big enough, I'd help with the pushing.

Mama loved the autumn. Do you remember walking to the zoo down Frome Road, while the plane trees undressed themselves for us? She would tell us they were taking off their royal cloaks to spread on the ground at our feet, because we were royalty too. She talked about autumns we would know nothing of, with squirrels and frosts and roasting chestnuts.

Who was it who asked the other night about chestnuts? I don't remember, must have been Katie, but I found one in one of Mama's 'memorabilia' shoe boxes. It had a string tied to it and it had gone grey and crinkly. What did she call them?

Anyway, here's next Xmas's present to us, a bit early, but it is going to last all year long. I'm going to scan all of the diaries, so I'm sending you each a copy to read as I get them done.

Love as always

Bella

4 February 2011

To: Bella, Jack

<u>Subject: Conkers!</u>

Conkers! She called them conkers. She and her cousin used to fight with them, trying to crack each other's chestnut. She said it was terrible just standing there holding up your precious chestnut for someone to smash with their own. It was like waiting for the dentist to take a tooth out, she said. Her cousin Tomas always won. I know! Let's roast chestnuts this winter. We'll buy lots and roast them on the barbecue at the Big House. Can you feel the whisper of the cold winds of autumn, just thinking about it?

I have a request: we're all busy at Christmas times and as often as we try to get together, it is still a complicated time of year. I know it's just passed, but how about this next Twelfth Night we all go through her box, together? Pleeease? The three of us – and our partners too, of course – if you want…so please make sure you have the time set aside. I know that Jack may be overseas again, but you can always Skype us. Or change jobs, of course… Or maybe just stick to one for a while…

Hugs and kisses

Katie xoxo

PS: Baby's the size of a lemon.

5 February 2011

To: Katie, Jack

<u>Subject: Hard task</u>

Hi All,

Great idea, Katie! We'll have a Twelfth Night like we used to. I've done some more scanning for you to read :) This is actually a hard task sometimes. It's as if she's leaning over my shoulder, like she used to. Do you remember? She would lean in and play with the hair at the nape of our necks, twirling it around her fingers. Or, because my study is in Pa's old study, I think of her as sitting in her chair watching him work, like she did at the end. Just waiting. Creepy. I keep remembering things as I read.

Sometimes I feel like we're eavesdropping, but after over fourteen years and five months – but who's counting – I think it's okay…is it?

'So', as Mama would say, what do you remember of her really? Do you remember the way her eyes flashed when she was cross? Do you remember how big her hugs were? The light of her smile? Her out of tune singing while she hung the clothes out or drove us around? Humming that Chopin piece out of tune – ALL the time? The stories she told us? How strong and alive she felt. Or do you only remember how grey and plastic her skin became; how hollow the sockets of her eyes were at the end, like her eyes were going to just slip back and never be seen again; or how her sweet, low voice became a bit slurred as speaking became harder like she constantly needed to refresh a parched mouth?

If we were asked individually, we would all carry something different of her in our memory. Then if you were to write everything down, from all of us, you would find a fuller picture, maybe a clearer picture than from just one of us; and then if you were to include all her friends who knew her as adults and Pa, who knew her as a lover, and her students who knew her as a piano teacher and her clients who knew her as the creator of their heirlooms, the picture would become even clearer, and maybe, just maybe, there would be glimpses of her that we would never have imagined.

We gave her a shape that was all our own, but that was only a small part of her life – no, a really big and probably her favourite most precious part – but not all of it. Does that make sense? I used to think of her only in terms of her being my mother – her diaries reveal a woman so much more than that – but she didn't stay around long enough for us to turn into friends, the way we have with Pa. Now, as a mother myself, I know that there's so much more to me than my mothering and so there must have been all these other parts to her, and I'm so sad to be missing that. You can see bits of it in her diaries, her observations and particular phrases and her oh-so-German 'So!' Funny, how we never really spoke German with her, although I still understand some. Such a big part of our family history and yet she only spoke English with us. Why? So many questions that will never be answered.

She won't see our children grow, and we won't be able to say, 'Now, I understand why you…' She won't look at us wisely and say, 'I know how you feel, but this too will pass,' and yet she is so much a part of who I am. Of who we are.

To have loved and to have been loved is her gift to us and her wish to us would be – I think – that we should live all the days of our lives.

Anyway, here's some more…

Love as always

Bella

PS: formal invite for Twelfth Night will arrive by real post.

6 February 2011

To: Katie, Bella

<u>Subject: Enough</u>

Really, Bella, if you're going to scan Mama's diaries, scan the things!
You're turning this into a psychobabble abuse. If you need to grieve,
go ahead, but do you have to get so carried away? I appreciate your
effort, but enough is enough.

J

PS: Darwin is hot, heavy, but work is fine.

7 February 2011

To: Katie, Jack

<u>Subject: WHOOPS</u>

I forgot the attachment. Thanks for that, Jack. Does that mean you read the email?

BTW, Jack, what do you mean when you say I'm abusive with all of this? How is it abusive? Don't you have memories you want to keep? Don't you remember her playing hide and seek with you? Or that time she somehow knew something was up, when you and Mollydog had gone down to the dam, remember? Molly hated water and somehow had slipped in, and you'd gone in to save her but ripped your leg open on some wire as you dragged her out. Mama carried you all the way home. I remember, because she started calling out for me from the orchard but she wouldn't put you down until she could sit with you on her chair to inspect the damage. You were so proud of those stitches! We had a stitches party and Pa raised a toast to you for saving Mollydog at great cost and peril. Captain Jack! That was just after she got sick the second time. Come on, there has to be something.

Anyway, so, here's some more of her diary. Here she is, whispering to us through her journals and her cardboard boxes of 'bits 'n' pieces'. I'll keep the box here until Twelfth Night. We can share it around then, if you want to, or you can have a peek when you come to family dinners. Her diaries aren't very consistent, which is funny because her calendars always were. Nothing happened in our house that wasn't on one of her family calendars in her strong, round handwriting.

Anyway, it starts with the first journal, which you already have the beginning of. I don't even remember her making that chest of drawers she describes, but I still have them. I may have relegated them to the garage, but they are still there. Sturdy and dinged in lots of places, but – I still have them. Do you remember any of this, Katie?

Love

Bella

PS: Warning: there's quite a lot of it. Fancy not having a mobile phone…

<u>Attachment:</u>

June 1982

So, bite-size pieces. I've stripped the paint. I think there were four enamel layers over that beautiful wood. Now I have to wait for Papa to bring his sander down.

Bella's cheeks are bright shiny red with pain and she's miserable. Thank God for teething gel and Panadol. I've discovered that she'll suck and chew on a wet flannel, so there are currently five of those in the freezer!

My poor piano hasn't been cuddled in three days! But my fingers haven't missed it a bit. They've been dancing over grains and shavings and Papa's hand tools. Shhh, don't mention this out loud…

6th

Well, no wonder little Bella was so miserable: she cut three of the four molars in a week! I AM EXHAUSTED. I've heard that there is a phenomenon called sleep, but it apparently is only for the rich, or male, or two-year-olds of our species. I remember a good night's sleep used to be sleeping in until nine or ten on a Sunday morning. Now, I feel a new woman if I had six straight hours of sleep in a row. I haven't touched those drawers or my piano for days.

10th

Well done, me! Steve took Bella out to his parents' place this morning and I sanded and dusted my beautiful drawers. There's something hypnotic about the movement of hand over wood. I remembered watching Papa as a child; sometimes he would cover my hands with his own and move the sander back and forth along the grain. His gentle voice would rumble in my ear, 'See, Elinor, it breathes…'

Ahhh, the smell of fresh wood. It has the same effect as that indescribable aroma of freshly brewed coffee and Mutti's casseroles. Yes. Something like coming home.

So, the first coat of varnish is drying, tomorrow the second, and tomorrow evening it will be in Bella's room. Then I can throw out the cardboard boxes I have stacked and taped together for her toys and clothes. First I shall stomp on those boxes and then I might have a ceremonial burning on the back veranda…can you roast marshmallows on a cardboard fire?

I'll let you know tomorrow…

11th

I put the second coat of polish on first thing this morning. Right now, I'm sitting at the kitchen table basking in my own glory. Bella was not at all excited about the prospect of waking up to a new set of drawers, despite my description of how they would change her life, but I am not dismayed. My opus magnum stands under her window in all its resurrected glory, and it's filled with fresh drawer liners and her neatly folded clothes. The bottom drawer is not so neatly filled with her shoes and a shoebox of socks. I arranged all her soft toys on the top. I LOVE IT.

Steven duly arose from his work to inspect, admire and express awe. One day we will buy a whole house full of brand-new furniture, but for now – I'll keep going for long walks around the neighbourhood. I played Chopin's Nocturne, Opus 8, all the way through before going to bed. I am alive.

PS: no marshmallows. The fire smelled dreadful, but looked great.

September 1982

14th

I have a new addiction. Papa dropped in soon after I finished the drawers. He was very kind, and gently pointed out a few divots in the wood that may or may not have been caused by my overzealous sanding. He patted me on the back and asked for a cup of tea. I think I passed, but I want another project! I watch the footpaths whenever we go walking or driving. It's almost an obsession. In fact, it has been five long weeks since I finished those drawers. I have been practising arpeggios for hours and chromatic scales just to keep my fingers and brain busy. I start with C major and work my way up and down the keyboard for a couple of octaves and then D, etc, then I move onto the minor keys and…

I have now got three more piano students. Young Riley's parents should be paying me danger money as well as piano fees. When he finished his lesson today, he thought he'd surprise me by showing me how he can stand on his head. Unfortunately, he thought that the couch was the best place to try it. Of course, our lumpy old couch isn't designed for gymnastics and I had visions of his neck bending at fatal angles as I turned around to watch his legs flailing around in the air. I just managed to catch him before he tipped off, but smashed my knee against the arm of the couch first. All for the love of music! His parents' love, that is, not his.

The money is helpful, though, and I am grateful for it, but I'm soooo tired of listening to the same songs over and over again.

Karen came around with her two little bundles and she loooooooves my new addiction; she looked at me with renewed respect as only a best friend can. This is how I looked at her when she graduated from uni.

March 1983

Autumn! Again – already!

My how the seasons pass! Almost a year! I'm not very consistent about this diary thing.

Anyway, biiig family celebration at Steve's parents. His brother Chris is here for a whole month with his wife, Jenni. I haven't seen them since they left to work overseas. She has long, silky black hair, just like the Schwarzkopf ad. She's so tall, yet so tiny, I have no idea how she actually managed to fit their baby in! She's always elegantly dressed and her make-up is flawless, not my idea of a chemical engineer at all. Her smarts are almost better than Chris's, but you wouldn't hear him say so. She and I are chalk and cheese. I feel like an elephant next to her. Maybe I should buy some make-up…

Little Charlie is two now. They've called him Charles, or Charlie, which is a great pity because I thought that would make such a nice girl's name if ever we had another…

Anyway, Charlie has gorgeous black eyes and quite fair hair. Imagine that! He has a gurgly laugh, but otherwise very quiet. My little elephant princess was a bit tumbly for him, poor lad, but they followed each other around for the whole day. It's nice for Bella to have a cousin nearer her age. They're almost exactly a year apart, which is eight years closer in age than Bella and my sister's two. I'm sorry it is only for a month, but still, we have a month. Peter and Betty are, of course, overjoyed, it was the first time they had their whole family together in one place for years, and Betty is loving time with another grandchild. They haven't seen Charlie since they went over to Malaysia for his birth.

I don't think they like living so far away from both their boys. Admittedly we are in the same state – and country – but Henley Beach may as well be Melbourne or London as far as 'dropping in' goes.

April 1983

Went to the zoo with Jenni, Betty, Peter and the kids. Chris went in to Steve's work to 'check things out'. Bella and I took the train in, which I'm ashamed to say was her first train ride!

It's autumn so the leaves are starting to change even though the weather is still quite warm and sunny. I pushed her past the Festival Theatre and was about to let her run on the grass when I remembered that a squillion ducks like to do that too and they are very free with their droppings! Bella was cross until we got halfway down Victoria Parade and there were enough leaves for her to kick. She looked so funny with her three-year-old body running up to each small mound of leaves with such purpose! You'd think she was shooting for a penalty goal in the FIFA World Cup. A couple of times her kicks were so hearty she overbalanced. I wish we had a video camera. It's moments like these you want so much to remember. I shall tell that story at her 21st, including the squeals of delight.

Anyway, we had a great, if tiring, day. I spent all of my piano money on entry tickets and buying lunch, but what a day to remember! Walking back to the station I pointed out the university grounds and told Bella that that was where Daddy and I went to university. She said, yes, she knew Daddy was very clever. I mentioned again that I had gone there too, and I used to learn the piano from a famous pianist and play in front of lots of people and they used to clap and think my friends and I were very talented. She nodded and kindly held my hand. Huh! She's only three and a half! How do children make these decisions so young? Maybe she's comparing her learning piano to me learning piano. Yes, that must have been it.

NOTE TO SELF: TAKE BELLA TO TOWN AGAIN BEFORE AUTUMN ENDS.

Chris and Jenni left today. Steve is quiet and sad. I think he really misses his brother. They've always been close.

October 1983

So, Diary, it's been a while. Have you ever been to the Lion's Mart on Shepherd's Hill Road? What a treasure cave is there! I found an old door with a latch instead of doorknobs. All I could see was a fabulous kitchen table minus legs! It's hard wood and just needs some sprucing up. And I know I can spruce.

The kind man helped me tie it onto the roof of the station wagon, but it meant having to get Bella out of the car via the front seat. Bella thinks I'm crazy but she's getting used to the odd scavenger hunt. She scrambled out through the front easily enough. Still, it was worth all the inconvenience. I'm going to make a table out of it. Can you see it? I'll strip it and coat it and buy some legs from the hardware store. Papa will show me how. I must ring him tomorrow to let him know what a treat I have in store for him!

I do miss playing the piano as much as I used to. There's a feeling like the angels in heaven have joined in when you and the rest of the orchestra or singers meld and blend and soar and dive. The notes disappear and music transforms us into creators. I bet God was singing just like that when Bhoof! – Creation became matter.

Listening to other students learn how to play doesn't quite compensate. Not even Ruby, who's doing exceptionally well in her exams. Overall, though, teaching piano is going well, it's my little business and is our 'Miscellaneous' fund. Every Saturday evening we sit down together and go through the week's expenses; not a single penny gets spent unseen.

I bank all my fees, minus a little pocket money. Each week, our account gets bigger and bigger. It's like watching vegetables grow from seedlings to juicy ripeness. Very satisfying.

Steve thought it would just be handy pocket money when I first started. The first two years it helped pay the bills every quarter, and gave me the odd cappuccino or two with Karen or Marley. I now have twenty-two students! Two years ago, it paid for our family holiday, this year we reached our $2,000 emergency fund. Next year…maybe the moon.

November 1983

God bless him! Papa brought his ute around yesterday and Mutti watched Bella while we went to choose table legs. It's been weeks since I bought the door. He thinks it's a great idea and we discussed woodgrain and heatproof finishes all the way there. When we got back, he had to go off to a job, but he left me his trestles and drill. Mutti continued watching Bella for me, while I spent a happy afternoon sanding and varnishing. I'll finish it off on the weekend. Then we can put our old one outside for outdoor parties. This will look perfect with all the higgledy-piggledy chairs. A good day's work and, at the end of it, I walked into a house, a bathed child, no dirty dishes and the smell of dinner wafting through the back door.

Nice. I wonder if this is how Steve feels coming home. And why does food taste so good when you haven't prepared it? My parents stayed to eat with us; Papa inspected my work and gave me some – um – constructive criticism.

Bella wanted a story about boats tonight at bedtime, so I told her one about a table who didn't want to be a table, he wanted to be a boat, so one rainy day when the house was empty, he slipped outside, turned upside down and sailed away. Bella wanted to have painted sails and she wanted to know how a table could slip outside. She is such a sharp thinker.

25 November 1983

It's my birthday! Twenty-nine! Twenty-nine. Twenty-nine. Shhh. Well, it was my birthday; the day is nearly over.

My whole family came over for dinner. It feels something like being held when your whole family come around to celebrate like this. My mother, my father, my sister – and her family. I feel settled when we're all together. Mutti cooked a beautiful dinner in my little kitchen and baked a cake which Bella helped to decorate. Bella helped me blow the candles out. As usual, we scraped the layer of icing off where her efforts could still be seen, and Mutti added fresh icing for the adults. What a team!

Steve and Papa bought me – pregnant pause – my very own power tools! Yes indeed, I am the proud owner of a router, a sander and a jigsaw, bandsaw, planer, drill and nail gun. Papa said this was to make more fine furniture out of junk. Junk! He laughs at me. But I've sold over $500 worth of fine furniture to friends in the last two months, and yesterday Karen rang to say a friend of hers loved her coffee table so much that she wants one too. Yes indeed, this certainly beats hopeful parents paying me to listen to their children practise piano once a week in my lounge room. Ahem. With a few notable exceptions who are actually delightful to teach and to know. Sorry, Karen.

My girl thinks it's very funny that her mother was given power tools for her birthday. So I told her a story about some power tools who secretly went on adventures and had parties when the garage door closed. She had to make up noises for each tool! It was so funny, and we made so much noise that Steve came in to see what all the laughter was about and joined in.

January 1984

I always start the year with a new diary; goodness knows what happens to Time in between the middle and the end of the year! What a waste of paper. Maybe, I'll stick photographs in them. Excellent idea.

So, the festive season came and went and I'm sure I didn't even blink! Bella really enjoyed her Christmas; we spent it with Steve's parents. There is an advantage to celebrating Christmas on Christmas Eve with my family. It was so funny this year! Marley's two had so much fun keeping all the magic for Bella. When Papa dressed the tree that night and invited us all into their sitting room for the lights to go on, they each held her hand, 'Wait, Bella, wait!' 'Watch, watch!' and, oh, her face as the lights came on the tree! Real Christmas trees, hand-made decorations and presents underneath… Of course, we can't light real candles on the trees any more, but Papa went around the room and lit candles. One for my sister and one for me and one for each of the grandchildren. When we were little, he would always pronounce our names in his deep, gentle, rumbly German voice, as he held the flame to the wick. I've always loved that. Marlene… Elinor… And then he and Mutti light their candle.

Now that we have families, he turns to us and includes each of our family members as he lights it.

Twelfth Night was just Steve and me. We took the decorations down one by one, listened to the Lemgoer Choir, drank wine and toasted the Christ Child, just as the Wise Men would have come to pay their respects. Next year, we think we'll have a party.

February 1984

Bella and I have started going to a playgroup at the kindy this term. We're both meeting new people; Bella gets to meet some children who'll be going into kindy with her next term. Wow! A big kindy girl.

The first week was a write-off, though: she had another ear infection, more antibiotics. Poor thing. She'd been so excited to go; she laid out all her clothes the night before. When she was too sick to go, we sat down at our little people's table and ate lunch at home out of lunch boxes to pretend we were already at kindy. She's not a bit nervous.

April 1984

My goodness, best friends have uses beyond watching your back, telling you when your skirt is caught in your undies and coming over for coffee during the day to remind you that adults exist in the world. I think I mentioned Karen's friend? Well, this friend has a friend who has an interior design business and they want to use some of my furniture for a catalogue to show off their soft furnishings and lamps etc! They asked me for my business details! Uh. So, quick-witted me just blurted out that I didn't have any and the only examples of my work I had were in my house. She's coming over anyway to have a look! At least, she said she'd ring me, but is that a case of 'Don't ring us, we'll ring you'? The endorsement is great, though. Funny, isn't it, how great it feels to be admired or appreciated for something you make? I hope she rings.

June 1984

Grommets have worked wonders. Bella is like a new child – or the original one back. Anyway, my little girl is much happier. Such tiny little devices that slip into such tiny little ears and all is well. I hated giving her up to the anaesthetist, though.

On a new note, I have a business! Yes, I do! Not with Karen's friend's friend. She hasn't rung. But wait! The kindy's having a fundraiser and I offered to take orders for shoeboxes, racks and coat racks. For samples, I took in the boot racks and coat racks I made for the back door, made out of floorboards from a wrecking sale. I'd found some old coat hooks at an antique store in Mannum and painted everyone's initials over each hook.

They match the initials of the boot rack. I have 26 orders! Busy, busy me! What fun! I'm charging $30 per piece and the kindy gets half. As a working business name, I'm going with 'Elie's Shed'. I even have a business name. Yes!

We threw a congratulations barbecue on the weekend. We had Marley and Simeon and their two. I must say I'm continually surprised that both Paddy and Michele don't look anything like our side of the family. Nothing hazel-eyed or mouse brown about my niece and nephew! All Sim: dark, dark Irish. Mutti and Papa, Karen, David and their girls came too.

Everyone brought a plate; we ate on our old table and some benches we salvaged from an old church sale. When we rescued the benches, Bella and I painted the old chairs different colours with the stressed look. My mother doesn't understand why anyone would want the pre-loved look in furniture or clothing. She told Bella she likes them, though, since she's so proud of them.

We set it all up under the carport and made little brazier fires. No rain and one of those bright winter days. Everyone stayed till it was time to turn leftovers into an early tea, the sun set, children bathed and in borrowed T-shirts. Except for Marley's two, of course, Michele and Paddy are a little past the snuggling into Uncle Steve's T-shirts stage! In fact, Paddy's as tall as I am now!

Later, when everyone was gone, little Bella tucked in bed, Steve and I sat outside around the last of the fires with cups of tea and talked over the day. It was such a lovely family day; our little house was bursting at the seams with family, children, games and laughter. Everyone pitched in. We even played backyard cricket and sang songs around the piano. The men admired David's new ute, Hi-lux thing. My shed was also duly admired after Steve reminded everyone that this was the cause for the celebration.

Bella had so much fun. As we were checking her for the last time before bed, Steve looked down and asked me if I sometimes wondered if there was someone missing in our family. This surprised me, but it is something I'd thought. So we think we might try for another little one soon. I don't know if I'm scared, excited or reluctant.

July 1984

I thought this kindy order would be easy, but I'm finding it quite difficult to fulfil. Anyway, I have a deadline now: I need to have the last ten completed by Friday. That's two and a half days. Where did the last month go? Papa is coming to help me tomorrow night after work. Bless his cotton socks.

August 1984

Done! The coat racks were a huge success. Elie's Shed is now a name. Karen and David came over for tea and Karen has convinced me to advertise in *Country Magazine*. So tomorrow I'm going to take photos of the back porch, David is going to play around with some business cards, and I'll write an ad for the local *Messenger*.

September 1984

Last night, I was lying in bed and thinking about Christmas. I want our children to have a tree house, which is a bit tricky because the only trees in our little backyard are fruit trees. But I think we could plan one to come off the side of my shed. I've worked out a way that we could build it in pieces and then put it together for Christmas Eve. I am so excited. I thought at first I could add this to Elie's Shed repertoire. Does furniture have a repertoire? Piano-playing furniture restorers can if they want to! But I'll see how tricky it all is.

This morning I woke up feeling very, very, very tired. Either I got up in my sleep and ran a marathon through the dark streets or I'm pregnant! Bit confused, because normally I'm throwing up every morning, noon and night. Too early to tell, maybe. I wish pregnancy tests were quicker. But how strange not to be sick! Great, but strange.

This weekend we're going to buy a garden shed for everything that's not to do with Elie's Shed. My shed is going to be my 'office'.

October 1984

Steve loves the idea of a tree house off the shed and immediately sat down and engineered some very good plans. I'm going to source some packing crates, or old timber. I want to run a slippery dip out of a window, so I guess it can't be too high!

The days have become a bit warmer and my vegie patch is looking good. Each little leaf and sprout so green and fine. There was plenty of blossom on the fruit trees this year, so I'm hoping there'll be lots of fruit. So far they're looking good. The lemon tree is as usual a faithful, fruitful contributor to my family and there'll be lots of lemon cordial this year again.

November 1984

So a pregnancy test from the chemist won't work for another week, but I woke up this morning to race to the toilet and vomit. I thought it was too lucky. Maybe I wasted my money. So there could be another little bundle next year late winter. Think of me smiling at the moment. I'm too tired to move my facial muscles.

MISERABLE BIRTHDAY SPENT OVER THE TOILET BOWL

7 February 2011

To: Bella

<u>Subject: family therapy</u>

Really, Bella, don't you think this reminiscing thing is getting a bit much? What are you wanting? A happy ever after story? This going through stuff that finished over a decade ago is a bit irrelevant now.

Unhealthy much? Maybe we weren't as close as you think we were in your head. These are your memories, not mine. I think it's time you moved on.

J

8 February 2011

To: Katie, Jack

<u>Subject: medical advances and mea culpa</u>

First let me say, Jack, that you have been championed by Katie and if you don't want to receive any more of Mama's diaries and my apparent raving, then let me know and I won't send them to you. That's not much of any culpa at all; you don't have to read it. I'm sorry that I've brought up bad feelings for you. Katie rang and told me in very Katie-like terms that I'm bordering on the self-indulgent.

Well, I disagree. We didn't really understand what the loss of her meant to us back then. Pa became busier and Oma was fantastic, but so matter of fact. I didn't know how to hold you all any better than Mama had taught us. Her tactic was to hold us and whisper in our ear that it might look bad, but she promised it would get better and that she would sit with us until it did. She didn't lie. She just didn't know then that some things don't get better.

Maybe this is just me, but if so, sit with me. Please. This is about us. You said, Jack, that maybe we were only close in my head. Did we lose our way then for a while? You've always been the strong adventurer of the family. I'm sorry if I lost sight of you. There has not been a day since you were born that I would not have beaten monsters to a pulp for you. But maybe you were the one beating monsters to a pulp... Sorry.

Moving on. If you want to. If not, press delete and exit.

Jack, if you're still reading you can put your fingers in your ears and sing 'La-la-la-la...' for a minute.

Katie, I wondered about the pregnancy test thing too. We can find out within days now, but I asked a pharmacist in Blackwood today and apparently they weren't accurate until about 8 weeks then. Can you imagine having to wait that long! Anyway, sickness didn't seem to stop her. She just used to keep going.

Miss you, Jack. How is hot and heavy Darwin going:)?

Love as always

Bella

BTW

Family tea is at Katie's this month, but she's not allowed to cook… she's feeling sick.

<u>Attachment:</u>

November 1984

So, the shed/tree house is going well. I bought some old packing crates, three of them. We put a raised roof over two lidless tops and the third will have a lookout. I carved two doors and one window out of all of them. Each one is going to be joined to the next by a cargo net. There'll be a slippery dip out of the middle one, a rope ladder to the highest one and a ladder up to the lookout on the lowest one. The highest one will be about a metre and a half and the lookout will be the same height as that roof. Clear? As mud. But we have the plans and it is going to look extraordinary. The best in Adelaide, the world even.

I'm going to have to plan my days now. I'm finding shopping and cooking very difficult to manage with morning sickness. Boys get it so easy. Walked past the deli section in Woolworths this morning and nearly didn't make it out to the car. Fortunately I had my trusty little bucket and hand towel waiting for me.

What was I thinking to go through this again? Oh, yes, I remember: another little person to welcome into our family.

December 1984

My, how the weeks fly by! I've had quite a few orders for Christmas, and I'm busy, busy, busy! These racks are my bread and butter, but I have a couple of rescue projects going on with furniture I've salvaged from roadsides, Lions marts, Goodwill etc. I might take a course in upholstery… These are the projects I love.

A few weeks ago, I took some samples of Elie's Shed around to the hardware store on Unley Road and Skinners in Blackwood and they're going to hold them and see if they get any orders.

School and kindy are gearing up for the end of year celebrations. This time next year I'll have two little bundles.

What a lovely weekend. We drove up to Belair National Park to the playground for a picnic. Marley, Sim, Michele and Paddy joined us and we all played for hours. Steve is so knowledgeable about the native plants and animals – not that we saw any animals, but he showed Bella evidence of where they'd been. We took a walk along a path beside the creek there and in the middle of the path was the most enormous oak tree! A truly, really oak tree with its old branches bowed over to the floor like one enormous green room. Bella loved it and I had a sudden ache to be living back in the hills with the European trees and the cooler weather and copious amounts of fresh, fresh air. Stirling isn't so far away from town and they say they're going to upgrade the Eastern Freeway. Steve isn't at all interested in moving; it's so convenient to be in Mitcham for his work in the city. Deep sigh. We shall just have to keep visiting my parents for my dose of country.

On Sunday night as I tucked Bella into bed, I told her a story about a faraway place where trees turned into castles and little girls into princesses and where the silly, little ordinary things in life become extraordinary, magical and full of fun. She wanted to know if there really are princesses. I thought maybe being loved made us princes and princesses, Steve came in and said she was his princess, so there must be. She wanted to know what made him so rich (we're living in a very small house in home-made clothes and shoes from Thrifty Footwear that fall apart after the second wear) and he told her that no matter how much money we had he would always be rich because he had us. That is such a lovely thought! She snuggled down very happily with his kisses on her forehead and a smile on her face. I just love this family-ness. Marley was always another parent for me. Our children will have each other. I wonder how it will be with another little one.

Saint Nicholas Day 1984

Saint Nicholas day! We went to Mutti and Papa's for dinner with Marley and Co. Paddy and Michele still walked around the orchard with their lanterns and held Bella's hand. There's no community to share this tradition with, nor darkened streets to be led around, no houses to knock on, and receive little sweets. I suppose we were too old for it when we moved here so we didn't miss it that much, but Mutti always hid treats around the orchard and backyard. It is lovely to watch our children enjoy the tradition.

Christmas is so soon. Lots of orders!

8th

Guess what? Our little primary school has a lantern walk every Carols Night that the kindy kids are allowed to be a part of! They play the Lantern Song, and Bella felt really proud that she already knew it. They play the song over the PA system and all the children take a lantern and walk around the oval. I nearly cried.

18th

All Christmas orders signed sealed and delivered! One week to go. It's useful to have Christmas Eve as our traditional Christmas, because that leaves Christmas day for Steve's family.

Steve took some time off this Christmas and Papa and Mutti came around so they could help with the cubby. The men fixed a pulley on Papa's ute to lift the crates into place.

It's a good thing that Bella isn't allowed in my shed very often! I'd have had a hard time explaining the cubby houses to her. She thinks the posts against the outside wall are for another garden shed. No one mentions how sneaky you have to get when you have children! Shocked, I am, but unrepentant.

I felt like an excited child, waiting for Bella to go to sleep that night. Steve kept laughing at me, and Bella thought it was all about Christmas coming and got excited too. I put carols on the new CD player to distract her. CDs have a fabulous sound and you don't have to keep rewinding the tapes or switching them over, you just press play! How amazing is that? LP's always sounded better than cassettes, but these CDs are great. I sort of miss that first crackle, though, as the stylus first touches the vinyl. Papa still prefers his records.

So eventually the crates were bolted to the platforms and the nets and ladders all attached. Mutti had made curtains for the windows and Papa made them a table and four little chairs to sit at. I want a set myself! It looks fantastic. Steve bought a whole stack of tinsel and ran a tinsel rope all the way from Bella's bedroom door to the bottom of the tree house ladder. We woke up to squeals and demands to wake up! She had already followed the trail, but hadn't gone inside yet. So we all trooped outside and pretended to be surprised to see what Father Christmas had done to our new garden shed! We decided that we would have to find somewhere else for the shed, but maybe this was a better idea anyway. Bella LOVED IT! And we loved her joy. Happy Christmas, little family.

3 April 2011

To: Bella, Jack

<u>Subject: Fancy!</u>

No phone to capture your moment of grace amongst the leaves, Bella! And you're right, how on earth did she survive without a phone? Looking forward to dinner. Nothing spicy please…

K, Brad and Bump

xoxo

3 April 2011

To: Katie, Bella

<u>Subject: dinner</u>

Darwin's a bit far for dinner, but thanks anyway. Hang on! Mama built that tree house? I thought it was always at the Big House. Work is fine, crunching numbers is crunching numbers, better than the job in Malaysia last year, my language skills made socialising harder. I don't mind the hot and heavy, actually, Bella :)

J

3 April 2011
To: Katie, Jack
<u>Subject: Tree House mystery</u>

Ha! Ha! So Jack, you thought the tree house was already at the Big House! Well, now you know. It was built for Katie and me and let me tell you it had PINK curtains to start with. Pink curtains and a pink and white table and chairs in the top room. I truly believed that fairies had left that tinsel and when I saw the tree house I was busting to explore it, but I was too scared there might be fairies still in it and I knew humans aren't supposed to really look at them. Later on, we were the envy of all our friends. Katie used to tie teddy bears to a pole on top of the lookout so that they could be on watch for dangerous animals.

Fortunately we grew out of the pink and white stage and Jack, when you were about two, we helped Mama paint the table and chairs in bright red, blue and green. Katie wanted the tree house to look like the work shed so Mama and Opa painted the fireman's pole and the window edges with the same red as the shed doors. Remember, Katie? Jack, you tried to play Superman out of one of those windows and discovered gravity is your kryptonite. Mama brought you home from getting your arm plastered and built window boxes in the sills and grew herbs in them so you couldn't climb out!

Thank you for your postcard, Jack. I really am sorry.

Love as always

Bella

FYI, Uncle Jack, Katie's tummy is quite round now :)

<u>Attachment:</u>

January 1985
HAPPY NEW YEAR! So here's a surprise. Do you remember Karen's friend's friend, the one who was interested in my furniture? Well, she came round the other day and she's still interested in featuring my furniture in her

next catalogue to set off all her soft furnishings and accessories! Her name is Sandy Something-or-other-Eastern-European. They're going to put it all outside in the garden and also in the tree house! How exciting and although she isn't paying me, she will advertise the furniture as a local business, with all my contact details, and I'm so excited! Karen's two and Bella are going to be the models. This is lots of fun! I'm going to hurry up and finish restoring the old ladders to hang Steve's grandmother's coppers from.

Oooh, this is going to be good.

Oh, by the way, the pregnancy's going just fine. I'm the same shape I was with Bella so, despite the fact the sonographer refused to tell me what we're having, I'm betting on another girl. Poor Steve. He'll be sooo outnumbered, but it's okay because Bella loves tinkering on the car and she loves to watch the football with him.

February 1985

You should have seen the crew that came around just for a brochure! Three people to move furniture from the house and shed, one to direct where it would all go and another to be told where to place the cushions, curtains, fabric, lamps and occasional table. So much fun. The photographer loved the tree house and wanted to order one, but I said it was too labour-intensive for my little one-man business. He couldn't get over the fact it's just little old me (well, let's face it, NOT so little old me) and my power tools. I told him I could give him all my sources and he could come around and I could show him how to put it all together. He didn't look that keen.

March 1985

Baby's growing well and I'm actually enjoying being pregnant again now that I'm no longer cooking dinner with one hand holding a towel over my mouth. Bella is storing up different names, like she has an actual choice, but it's lovely to include her in the process.

I've just sold a whole lot of furniture, thank you, Sandy. Thank you, thank you, thank you! I've bought brand-new baby stuff with my hard-earned money. Took it and spent it all on me – well, Baby Bump, but that's for me. The catalogue Clayton's advertisement has been surprisingly and gratifyingly successful!

I'll finish teaching piano at the end of this term if Elie's Shed keeps growing. I must say that'll be a bit of a relief. Maybe I'll start playing again for myself. I've actually stopped enjoying it and Chopin and I have had a temporary separation.

Where did the last few months go? And how little time have I spent pondering this pregnancy and following each weekly growth? The miracle of human life in utero. I just know it's magnificent autumn for a couple more months and any time now a new baby.

Nothing personal, little one, I still can't wait to hold you, name you, learn you.

Must take Bella to Frome Road sometime in the next few weeks or all that golden debris will be gone. So many delights and so little time. And no energy for anything after children, furniture and household chores.

April 1985

Bella's first day at school and she was so excited. Her primary school invited the following term's intake to have one morning a week at the big school. Such a good idea, don't you think?

I like the way all the primary schools in Adelaide teach a foreign language. Our primary school teaches German. I guess that's because of the rich German history here, and goodness knows my parents are keen, but wouldn't an Asian language be more useful to them in life?

All the exciting things to learn and join in with the big kids! Six of her kindy friends have joined her at the primary school, some have gone off to private schools. Next term we're going to take the baby in for show and tell. Bella looked so grown-up in her uniform. I was cheerfully waved goodbye, and so it happens. The next stage complete, a new one begun. And I get five hours a day for a couple of months to finish all this furniture.

Yesssss.

May – sometime

I haven't watched *Play School* today so I can't even tell you what the day is, let alone the date!

So several false starts and a brand-new baby! You'd think I'd have worked it all out the second time around but she was so totally different, which I think is going to be a reflection of her personality. A head full of chestnut hair and a fantastic pair of lungs! I just wish she'd sleep more. Katherine Jean, Katie, Katie Jean – any way you say it sounds good. 7lbs 6oz, on 13 May 1985. Our brand-new baby girl.

Reluctantly, I'll have to put work on hold for the next couple of months, but I'm just itching to get back into it again. I've been rescuing bits of furniture, which is frustrating the family a bit because it's piling up under the carport against the house and it's threatening to curtain the girls' bedroom window. I'd put them in my shed, but it's – um – I did manage to build floor to ceiling built-in cupboards in the girls' room before Katie arrived. Little Katie is in a bassinet in our room at the moment. Tomorrow. I'll do it all tomorrow…or tomorrow's tomorrow…

July 1985

My, how time flies when you're having fun! Little Katie is in a really useful sleep pattern, which should last another couple of months, and Mutti comes down two afternoons a week to help me when Bella gets home from school. Katie and I pick Bella up from school and admire all her schoolwork, anecdotes, then listen to reading until Mutti arrives and they play all afternoon. I've only just realised how fortunate I am to have such young parents with time to spare me, and how fortunate the girls are to have such young grandparents. Fortunate and grateful.

So my brain is returning and I have several pieces of furniture in various guises and in varying stages of completion. Sandy has kindly agreed to stock my furniture in her interior decorating shop. She takes a percentage of the sale, so my prices have gone up and, oddly, they're selling better at higher prices! Why do you suppose that is? So our battered-up cars can take refuge under the carport once again, and the lovely smell of wood and lacquer and stain are all through my shed, and hair and clothes. Mmmn.

August 1985

Chris and Jenni have just had a baby girl, Lauren Anne. Another cousin, but none to play with.

Katie's twelve weeks old and I swear she's cutting teeth – can babies cut teeth at twelve weeks? Oh sleep, sleep, but she's doing all the hard work, poor love.

13th

Yep. Babies can cut teeth at twelve weeks and no days old. Every sleepless night seems to wear me down so much. Every time she gets a tooth, I get a cold. Talk about sympathy pains.

Grrr.

November 1985

So time passes on, this shifting sand, ticking clock, sun up, sun down. Another year gone.

We're in the middle of baking gingerbread biscuits. Mutti came over armed with her beautiful cookie cutters and away we went. Every year I've been decorating the tree with gingerbread hearts and trees and buying one special decoration. If my business keeps going the way it is – and let's face, it people always need furniture – next year, I'll be able to buy any decoration I want.

Advent begins tonight and Bella will light the first candle. Next year Katie will do it the second week. With some assistance from Mama. Saint Nicholas Day in two days' time.

Marley's two are organising a concert together with Bella, but they haven't agreed on who the producer is yet. I even suggested one producer and one conductor, but that didn't help them at all. They have agreed on a list of carols, though. That has to be good, right? Karen came over with her two the other day and her two gentle souls just looked at ours and took the discretion-is-the-best-part-of-valour path. They've been included in the concert and very politely agreed to all the many and constant changes in direction. Karen and I just fed them fritz sandwiches and apple quarters.

Bedtime stories are much more fun now. I do enjoy Christmas time stories, and more so since we added the Oak Tree Palace. I can take them through countries now and not just imagination. Bella is adding her own bits and sometimes we take it in turns. Every time Katie babbles, I translate her suggestions. Steve just comes in and listens when he's home in time, which isn't so often these days. Apparently this is what happens when you work for promotions. But sometimes he makes it and lifts the girls on to his lap and snuggles them; or he lies down on Bella's bed and falls asleep. The girls giggle and he pretends he was listening the whole time when we wake him up. I think he recharges his batteries that way. They do miss it when he's not there for bedtime.

We went late-night shopping the other week and ordered the girls a trampoline! I am so excited. Steve took ages choosing it, researched sizes, dimensions, quality of steel, springs, mats. He's dug a hole in the garden, which he'as told the girls is for a barbecue he wants to build. This way, the trampoline can be sunk into the ground. It will be the most engineered trampoline in the whole of Australia.

The house is feeling smaller as Katie becomes more and more a personality. We have two such happy bundles, we're so blessed. I'm enjoying having Katie all to myself during the day. It's like having just one again for a little while – well, one and a growing business.

You know, sometimes I feel really guilty asking for money because I just LOVE my job. Insert happy skip here and really wide smile. Not that this will stop me charging for all my hard work.

I look down the ages sometimes and know that this is a great time of life. Steve and I are young and have all our dreams in front of us; we have two lovely little girls and work that we love. We shall live well all the days of our lives, just like our bedtime stories.

7 April 2011
To: Katie, Jack
<u>Subject: Bumps</u>

Mama calls babies Bump too! Did you notice that? How weird is that…?

xxx

Moving on, I know that there's a lot in there about before you two arrived, but it is still part of her diary.

I want us to have it all. Because this was her journey and I want to know what she felt, who she was – our world through her eyes. I guess you don't have to read everything and maybe some things will be intimate, Jack, but we can't just choose what parts of her to like. There's a big jump in time now. She didn't keep a diary for a whole year. She had a lot on her plate.

Katie, I know what you mean about feeling her close in your pregnancy. These are the times I physically ached with missing her. Oma was great and talked to me about Mama's pregnancies, Marley too, but she was so different from Mama, as different as two sisters could be. Oma would remember how sick Mama would be, and the way she would rub her tummy and talk to the baby as it grew. How lucky we are that Mama's parents were so young! Opa's back is still straight and strong and Oma still has that twinkle in her eye. Our children will get to know them too. They were the ones still strong enough to step in at the end. They're here as we bring our own families into the world. Mama can't share in feeling that first kick or cry with Pa as they hold our newborn children. But they are here and we are here... Katie's babe, I can't wait to meet you.

Jack, who is this Jessica (presumably she speaks English) you keep mentioning and when are you arriving back in Adelaide? Are you still only taking on short-term projects?

Here's more.

xoxo

May 1987

Well, it's been a while, and it's not even New Year's Day. Chris and family are finally coming back to Adelaide. This will be great for everyone. We haven't seen them for four years now and the girls are so excited to have more cousins around. At least I hope they'll come around. It'll depend on where they end up living.

Big earthworks at our house! We're digging up the front yard to put a semicircle driveway with a carport at each end for our cars and at the end of the old driveway we've extended my shed and added more bench space for my business. We're also putting on a big back veranda to help with usable living space. This means, of course, that the fruit trees have been pruned radically and that the trampoline has been transported to the vegie garden. We'll just have to buy our vegies now, but the girls live on that trampoline.

At least Steve and I are both doing paperwork at night together now – a shared activity. We pour a glass of wine – or two – and work and chat. So romantic! Steve has instituted a once-a-month Friday Date Night. Sometimes the girls go up to Stirling for the night and we just go home and – crash.

Sometimes it's so hard to find energy for each other at the end of a busy day or week or month. Saturday mornings are much more fun, though, when it's just the two of us…

Last year, we put some advertisements in *Country Magazine*, and just like the catalogue two years ago, the business took off again.

One of Steve's colleagues, Neville, took early retirement, but misses work. He and his wife, Jean (what a lovely name), had come round for dinner a few times and he and I would go to the shed and talk tools and wood and restoration. Last September he turned up one Saturday and offered to lend me a hand with some pieces and he's been on the payroll ever since.

16th

I couldn't face setting and clearing the table tonight so we had a picnic on the trampoline, all rugged up in jumpers. Such fun! Such mess! I ache everywhere. Maybe I'm getting the flu?

June 1987

We're planning another baby. A planned addition, but I made a formal request that we start looking for a bigger place. Apart from my business, Steve's on a much better wage and convenience isn't going to make up for the occupational health and safety issues associated with overcrowding! I think I'd like a dog too. Every child needs a dog.

Bella's old enough for Saturday morning sport now, so we've just added another couple of activities to the week. Katie jumps from foot to foot on the sidelines cheering and has to be held on to because she has a tendency to fall off benches, prams, anything at all really. But always enthusiastically.

Sundays are still family days. We all love it; we go for picnics, walks, the beach in summer, Mt Lofty House gardens in any weather, Belair National Park. We still love the Oak Tree, and the girls always run off to wait for us there. We have to stand and pretend to knock and ask the princesses of the Oak Tree Palace for permission to pass.

December 1987

Not starting a new diary next year. So six months and no baby. But lots of work. Too much. I'm not keeping up and something is gonna give. I have an ominous feeling that it'll be me.

I'm still so tired. I'm getting enough sleep, but I wake up sluggish! I get the girls off to school and kindy and then come home and crash. It's like being pregnant, but without the morning sickness. That's how it was with Katie. Maybe I'm pregnant already! Either way, this is the last Christmas with just the four of us. I hope. Next year we'll be five. What a lovely quirky-shaped number...not as round as six! I think that would just be gluttonous. I feel greedy enough.

Bella thinks we should have a boy and she's busy with little boy names. She has a crush on a boy called Jared, so guess what name is top of her list? Me, I think we're just so good at little girls. On the reality side, Elie's Shed is going so well that we've employed my nephew, Paddy, to help us on Saturdays. He works while we go to sport and then he goes off to his own football match in the afternoon.

June 1988

Well, hasn't it been a while. I have a puppy! I have a puppy – well, of course, I mean WE have a puppy. She's a beautiful bitzer, black, pretty, gentle and totally adorable. There was an advertisement at the shops for puppies. We went round and this little one just ran straight up to Steve and plonked herself on his shoes and promptly fell asleep. Done. I know this might show she might be HIS dog, but actually it was just a bit of clever psychology on her part because he didn't want a dog at all. He just took one look at her and smiled. A bit like he did when the babies were born. Her name is Molly, but Bella keeps calling her 'Mollydog'. I think the name is going to stick, because even Papa calls her that and Steve, too if he's not on guard.

It's almost as good, but not really, as having a baby. Maybe she will be enough. Still not really recovered from that virus I had. Maybe I have chronic fatigue syndrome. Can you treat that? Mutti says I just have chronic fatigue and that I'm trying to do too much. Ha!

September 1988

I don't write much, do I. Statement. No question. No baby. All is well with Elie's Shed, but not Elie. Too tired. Too busy. Children are well. Steve is ridiculously busy. Too busy. Could explain the no baby.

1 May 2011

To: Katie, Jack

<u>Subject: First sadness</u>

It's strange reading this from her diary. This was a scary time for Katie and me. We used to lie awake at night or hop into each other's bed and whisper about it. All the grown-ups thought they were protecting us by keeping facts from us, but we knew it was serious. Somehow, by playing their game, we felt like we were protecting them. Katie would make up stories about fairies with magic potions that could heal anything. I'd stroke her hair, like Mama did, and whisper that it would be okay and I wouldn't let anything bad happen. Pa wouldn't let anything bad happen, because he was the king. Sometimes we'd sit out on the trampoline until really late and make magic potions out of different leaves in the garden. They always had nasturtium leaves in them because Oma said that they're very good for the health. Mama would smile and pretend to take them.

I can't imagine what it must be like to go to the doctor thinking that you only have a silly cold – again – to find yourself suddenly in a hospital bed and facing a hellish future. I can't imagine the agony of not being able to be the mother my children need me to be, or let go of the dignity of managing my own body. Losing myself piece by piece to disease.

I thought if I behaved better, she'd get better. That my behaviour could affect her illness. I used to worry that I had caused it. I was so scared of doing something wrong in case she died! Whoever said children are too dumb to be told the truth was never a child.

Love as always

Bella

May 1989

Saw your light on and thought I'd drop in! How long is it since we last talked? Well, since I last talked at you.

Still no baby. Life is so busy now. I fall in to bed every night and get up late every morning to hit the deck running. Steve drops the girls off to school and I disappear into my treasure shed. We have a great routine, who'd a thunk it? Elie, organised! It's more my friend and saviour every passing day. Everything's laid out for the morning before we go to bed and everything has a routine by what day it is. But every morning seems to be punctuated by grumbles, eager children forgetting essential school items, their lunch, their shoes, or not so eager children refusing to get dressed before tumbling into the car.

Katie has twice been driven to kindy in her pyjamas! I will mention that I did have her clothes with me. What a temper! She must get that from her Tante Marley; thank goodness only Bella's old enough for sport. Some of their friends at school are doing something every day! When do they get to live and play?

We're still in our little house, which is bursting at the seams! Literally. The back veranda now has sliding doors and has become the meals and living area. I keep our office stuff in the old little study, but we still like to work together on the dining room table. Well, the nights he comes home, we do. Mostly, it seems, I sit there until he comes home. Or I go to bed and he wakes me to say goodnight. I cannot shake this tiredness.

I love that table! We've had such happy meals around it. A few not so happy, but that's part of the glory and mess of family. Well, my family.

The trampoline has become another room; the girls take their homework, craft, books, snacks etc. out there. They sometimes sleep out there during the holidays. I can hear them whispering – or not – on the night air. Lots of insect repellent! Molly loves it too.

Chris and family have moved to Sydney. How bizarre it was finally living in the same state, but only getting together for significant occasions a couple of times a year. Steve and Chris used to play golf once a month, so he'll find this the hardest. I can't imagine not catching up with my family regularly.

Business is doing really well and we have clients from all over the place now. The Shed is always full and busy. I've employed a third person for all the delivery and collection of stuff. His name is Tim and he knows a lot about furniture removal! Neville helps me breathe new life into the furniture or 'bits of pieces' as Bella calls the timber. Paddy still works about ten hours a week. Mutti still comes over two afternoons a week and Michele comes over with Paddy sometimes, so I can play with the children while she puts the dinner on and folds clothes. No ironing happens round here any more. Well, that's not true. Steve has turned out to be a great work shirt ironer! Sunday is everyone's day off. The girls wrote a list of Sunday outings for the term and we have fun ticking them off the list.

Still no baby.

3 June 1989

So I've made an appointment with Dr McDonald and asked for some blood tests. I love having had the same GP as a child and now, and have him know my children. It's a family thing.

Marley thinks my thyroid needs checking; Karen has me on echinacea. Mutti thinks I'm just run down. Let's see what the doctor says. It's been so long now, of feeling glum.

Maybe I'm just sad that I haven't got pregnant. Maybe two lovely girls is all we'll ever have – oh yes, and one Mollydog.

11th

Um, so not so good. I'm not run down, I have lymphoma. I went to Dr MacDonald, and he talked to me about everything, like he does, astrophysics, literature, the children – one by one. Then he asked me what he could do for me today. He listened and poked and prodded and sent me off for blood tests. I thought it was for glandular fever or my iron levels, to show I had an exhausted immune system or something. Normally, blood tests take a few days, don't they? Well, he rang me back himself, the next day, and I was in hospital that night.

He was so sorry. I wonder how many children he's known all their lives, followed into adulthood and had to be responsible for telling them that their lives are just about to explode forever. He was positive, talked about treatment, possibilities and investigations. I just sat and listened without listening. I asked what needed to be done next, thinking I'd prepare for more tests, like you do for an induced delivery. You go home, cook a few meals, write a few lists, play with the kids, tell them how exciting it all is and wander into hospital a few days later with your little suitcase.

Not me. He told me to ring Steve, cancel my day, have the kids picked up from school by my mother, and that he'd already made appointments at Flinders Medical Centre for me.

And that is that. I can't write about this. I'll try later. I might be going to die. Am I going to die? What if I die?

I have lymphoma. Take four lives, throw them in a kitchen wiz, press blend. Thank God there was no baby.

July 1989

So here I am sitting in Flinders for another chemo session. Where did we last get up to?

I asked Dr Mac to ring Steven's work. Poor thing, he was in Perth at the time. I rang his PA to get the phone number of the office in Perth. Dr Mac then rang there, pulling Steve out of a meeting. Steve took the next plane back.

I rang Mutti before leaving for Flinders. It was a crazy conversation. True family colours: I stated the facts, she repeated them. I could tell she was writing them down; it would have been with the soft pencil and scrap paper she cuts up into A5 size and keeps clipped with an ancient bulldog clip by the phone. One piece for each message. She would have written the date in the top right-hand corner. In between my information she just exhaled, 'Mein Gott, mein Gott.' Nothing more. Papa left work so that he could be home for when the children arrived. Mutti picked them all up; they were expecting her because I'd rung the school to let them know, but they didn't know why. I asked for nothing to be said until we had a better idea.

I was immediately matched for blood types and prepared for a transfusion. Steve went back to the children later that evening.

14th

So I'm home now. Stories get read or told and then reread and retold. Stories that capture the imagination and transport you into a place that's enough like our own that we can feel at home there and so different that we can turn frogs into princes, ordinary everyday mundane life into extraordinary, unique adventures. I used to tell the girls stories like that and they'd ask for their favourites and we'd change them a little to slip in the real day we'd just had. I can't change this fairy story for them. Every day retells itself in all its ugliness and uncertainty. I start them, because they ask for them – then usually I fall asleep first! Bella and Katie take up the story if I get too tired. Usually Katie. Bella is very quiet. Steve has started to join us and he sits on the floor with Mollydog and fills in the gaps.

Haven't been out to the Shed in ages. I'm going to take up share trading, I think. Something I can do from my bed.

It's been six weeks since we found out my diagnosis. Six weeks and our world will never be the same. The type of lymphoma I have is treatable, but has a high chance of returning sometime down the track. Down my track. Thank God I didn't have a third child!

I'm now going through my fourth lot of chemotherapy. I always had this idea of chemotherapy as painful and feeling sick all the time. I'm not going to be that way apparently. I feel juuust fine. Well, comparatively speaking.

We struggled with what to tell the girls. The chance is definitely there that this could be a bit nastier than we think, but why cross that bridge until we have to? We ended up telling them that I have a bug in my blood and that I have to take some very strong medicine to get rid of it. The medicine is so strong that my hair might just fall out in shock!

They seem pretty resilient about it. Sometimes Bella gets this worried look on her face, but cuddles and distraction seem to be still working.

August 1989

My hair is falling out! I'm not the daintiest woman in the world, my frame is from large, good Saxon stock, I don't pretend to be beautiful, I've never spent hours at the hairdresser or over my clothes – but to have no hair!

I'm a monster being eaten by little cells that are being eaten by chemicals. I'm being eaten alive.

16th

Steve and the girls took me out shopping for hats and scarves today. I have no eyebrows but I have three hats and a hundred million scarves. All chosen and approved by my family.

They loved it. I hated it. I felt like a puppet, but the girls were so sure this would make me feel better and they were trying so hard to cheer me up. I want to curl up. I understand people wishing they had never been born.

23rd

Dear Neville, he's taken over Elie's Shed. He and Tim have slowed things down a little bit, but are keeping us all going. I can't manage the smell of the shed.

Mutti comes around and does the kindy school pick-up; she then stays and helps me with the evening meal, while I try to stay energised for the girls until bedtime. They've been so good, really; maybe too good. I think Bella is storing it all up until she can explode. Katie's just cheerful and self-contained as usual but throws the odd temper tantrum to let me know that all is as it should be. She's still a little on the clumsy side. Well, a lot actually. But she bounces so well and so cheerfully that it all becomes a part of her charm. She has a great imagination. She's had a bit of a rough time at kindy. Our lovely kindy that Bella went to. Mind you, there are new teachers there now. Only one of them I recognised.

I've had a lot of time to think about what the girls will be when they grow older. Will I see them grow older? Bella's going to be a hundred special things, like an astronaut, a world-famous artist, a writer or a maths teacher. She sings all day and she's composing songs on the piano. Her hair has turned darker and thicker and she refuses to have it tied neatly, except when she plays the piano, then she plaits it down her back like mine and tucks the fly-away strands behind her ears. Go figure…!

They're both really good at maths. They must get that skill from their dad because it does NOT come from me. They're both active and very vocal and neither one of them is an Indian. We have four chiefs in our family and this makes being one of the Big Chiefs very difficult.

Will I see my girls grow up? Will I watch them become who they want to be, watch their dreams come true, hold them when their dreams go bad? Watch them hold children of their own? Who will hold them when their dreams go bad?

When will Steve come home? So glad there was no baby.

November 1989

If you'd told me six months ago that I could be facing such terrible possibilities, I would have laughed in your face. If you'd asked me what I envisaged for the future, I would have looked down the ages and thought how much fun it's always going to be. No rose-coloured glasses, though. I would have wondered what my children would tell me when I'm old and grey and they're trying to bring up children of their own. I wonder if any of them will play music, or love wood, or will they be engineers, like Steve and Chris and Auntie Jenni and build things. I looked down the ages and I could see Steve and me sitting in our Jason recliners watching a tribe of grandchildren tumble and grow, like our own children are growing. I believed we had a beautiful shining on us. I would have acknowledged that parenting is exhausting, expensive.

Now, as I recover from all this treatment, my outlook is a little different and sometimes the sun is definitely NOT shining on us. I lose my voice yelling. Katie's withdrawing further away and Bella's trying to run the household at nine years old. It's true, occasionally, they turn into monsters and I have to go play the piano to stop my fingers from turning my children into statistics! Aarrgghh! But Chopin always comes to my rescue; it doesn't matter how traumatic all this is, he's always there for me, like a lover, or an elixir. I can close my eyes and my fingers take over. To touch the keys is to be healed. It's even better than the feel and smell of the wood under my hands. So why don't I play more? On my bad days I just fill the house with CDs and the girls go outside to play.

Those times when emotions get a bit high inside the house, they go outside and sit on the trampoline which is the designated 'Mama keep out' zone. I can see them now from my chair, their heads together talking or jumping about, until we all get over it and mostly our little house is okay.

This mothering bit can be sooooo hard sometimes. All this treatment doesn't make it easier. We're trying so hard for the girls, trying to be a family. Reading up on how to help them. There's a bit around on what to do after someone dies, but not a lot about when parents are sick. Although I am responding well to treatment. They don't talk about that much in the books, do they? And somehow, you don't remember your parents having bad days. Will they even remember this time? Have there been enough good days for this time to be just a shadow of a memory. I do so hope so. Just a shadow of a memory in our family.

At night the ritual is still goodnight stories. We all pile into one of the girls' beds and I tell them another story about our castle under the oak tree. I do love oak trees. I remember parks of them when I was a child. It's summer and sometimes we all climb on to the trampoline after baths and teeth and stay up a bit later than usual. The problem seems to be that the older they get, the more alarming and repulsive the stories have to get.

The favourite repulsive part of every story at the moment is fart bombs. Last night, it was so loud and so gaseous that the castle actually shot into orbit leaving a crater in the yard where it used to be. The castle family circled Earth a thousand times before landing upside down. Everyone in the castle had to climb up to the cellars (dungeons haven't appeared yet) to avoid getting crushed. It was a lot of fun. They both add their own contributions to the stories now. I've decided that I have very verbally talented children, the downside being that sometimes there's no off button to be found. Katie adds the grossest details.

At least I can still tell stories. I know! From now on, I shall write the stories down, so if ever a tomorrow doesn't come they can still tell each other stories.

11 November 1989

So the world gave me for my birthday a whole new era. The Berlin Wall has fallen! Mutti rang me in tears. It's true. The Berlin Wall is no more. There was footage on the news of people clawing at the wall, climbing to the top and ripping pieces off. Guards were just standing by. Last week, they would have been picking them off like flies in a staccato of bullets, leaving their broken bodies in the no-man's-land to join all the plaques of others who dared to try for freedom. Papa is very quiet and Mutti is writing a lot of letters. What will happen now? All those mercy packs that my Oma used to send to her friends across the Wall, all that welfare. What will it mean?

26th

Last tests and appointment tomorrow! I'm very confident. I've shown a great response to the chemo. And the winner is…

27th

Elie! Elie is the winner. I told you I'd be all right. Seems that my family has me until I'm old and grey. Steve cried and my family and Steve's parents came over for a celebration.

I just wanted to be quiet somewhere with my little family. Tomorrow. Oh, and tomorrow and tomorrow and all the other tomorrows.

Happy Birthday to me, Happy Birthday to me. If I had the energy, I'd dance a happy dance! Next year.

27 April 2011

To: Bella, Jack

<u>Subject: Adelaide</u>

So, Jack, you're moving back to little old Adelaide! Just in time for your little niece or nephew, who is now the size of ULURU!

I got goosebumps when she wrote she was the winner. What a 'horrible, terrible, no good' night she must have had the night before.

Katie xoxo

PS: What happened to the music, Bella?

27 April 2011

To: Bella, the uterus of Uluru

Re: Adelaide

Yep. Gonna give Adelaide a go. Not sure what I'll do, but I didn't renew my contract here. Will ring. So when did my niece/nephew change from vegetable to mineral?

J.

28 April 2011
To: Katie, Jack
<u>Re: History Interrupts</u>

Hello All,

Interesting you should ask, Katie. I'm about to sit down with my cello for the first time since, well, since Mama died, I suppose. And Jack, it's Katie's uterus we're talking about, so really anything could happen.

Another big gap. Really big gap. You know, I've never thought much about how world changes must have affected Opa and Oma, and so Mama. I've found a newspaper clipping about the fall of the Berlin Wall; she must have cut it out. Do you even know what it was? She doesn't talk much about it, but she crossed out three blank pages in her diary in red ink after it. She doesn't mention friends she knew when she was a child. Actually, she doesn't have anything much from before they moved to Australia. I wonder why? Maybe Oma would tell us. Then again, maybe not. Maybe I'll speak with Tante Marley – she was so much older than Mama, she might know. Do you think they were as close as siblings as we all are? I wonder if the age difference mattered much when they were in their thirties. A ten-year age gap can mean so much when you're little. That's about the same difference between Michele and me, which is probably why she and Paddy seemed more like grown-ups rather than cousins.

Anyway, back to her ramblings. She loved autumn, and now I love it because she did. I remember her bending down to crinkle leaves in her hand; or at Mount Lofty, on our walks, she'd suddenly stop and open her arms out wide as if one of us was about to jump into them, and take huge breaths of air. I can almost hear her trying to shoo us all into the car for a trip to Mt Lofty to make cubbies in the leaves.

So, Jack, you have a new hobby? My Madi and Jackson love the rocking horses and think their Uncle Jack is the best uncle 'eva'!

You have a newly awakened talent. Or should that be 'reawakened' talent? It was a great package to unwrap.

Thanks, Katie, for the phone call, I'd forgotten that she used to go out and say goodnight to all the vegetables before she went to bed at night. She must have missed her vegie plot in the old house, but what a great idea that trampoline was! Do you think she used to go out to the shed to touch all the furniture and say goodnight? I bet she did!

Katie, I found a whole lot of your early work here. Another memorabilia box. She'd written 'Katie's Masterpieces'. I tried ringing – but your phone is always off. You okay?

Like I said last time, it's not the first story I remember, though. She always began them the same way. I liked that – it added to the anticipation.

Sometimes she wrote pages, sometimes a line or two and sometimes nothing for months and later years. Why do you think she kept on writing? She kept a whole stack of calendars, though. 2 p.m. dentist/dance concert/Steve – Melb/Jack's grand final! etc.

Katie, I know what you mean about your autumn walks, I took Madi and Jackson down Frome Street last autumn and they both ran straight for the piles of leaves and all the uni students just walked on by. It was so much fun. We're going to go again next year and the year after that etc. Why don't you come too? You'll have a little bundle to bring by then. How great is this going to be? All our kids will have cousins they can play with. Paddy and Michele were like adults to us. Charlie and Lauren were great whenever they came back to Adelaide, but that wasn't often enough. New adventures for a new generation. Not you, Jack – you can wait a few years yet...

Love as always

Bella

March 1990

Now that it's here again, I think that autumn is such a beautiful time of year. Think of how much life there's going to be, lying dormant for a few months before exploding into spring.

What an amazing gift to tomorrow these dying leaves are: mulching, composting foliage, the fallen petals and the crinkled, crackly lush of summer. So Elie's Shed hasn't really survived the chemotherapy. Sales are down, which makes sense since that was my task. Have had to let Tim go, the hardest thing I've had to do – ever. But I haven't been paying myself – and so my family – for four months now, just to keep him on. We talked about it a couple of months ago and I said I'd keep him on until he started a new job, so he knew it was coming. Fortunately, he's found something. We had a farewell barbecue with Neville and Jean, Tim and his new girlfriend and my family. Bit sad really. But the backyard looked fantastic. Steve put up fairy lights with great precision and engineering and set up braziers.

I'm really going to start writing down our bedtime stories now that I'm well enough to start them again.

No house yet.

July 1990

Still no house. But wait, it gets better: apparently two methods of contraception are not enough to prevent pregnancy... Guess what, though? Pregnancy tests from the chemist can tell you within a couple of weeks now! How amazing is that?

So that bug that was going around the girls' school that they brought home, the one I thought – in true Mum fashion – I'd managed to avoid but succumbed to soon after, was more than just a bug. The doctor says that the baby should be fine despite the last year, but I'm still concerned. I feel cheated. I so wanted another child and the joy and anticipation of pregnancy. Now I'm too worried to enjoy anything.

Have no idea when she – or he – is due, but Steve has an appointment with our GP next week.

Steve is sore, but stoic!

28 April 2011

To: Katie, Jack

<u>Subject: More read, no comments</u>

Lots of love

Bella

PS: Have begun writing my own memories down for Madison and Jackson. My own Memory Box.

<u>Attachment:</u>

October 1990 and spring is in full swing

Every pregnancy can be remembered by projects accomplished. The last few weeks I've tried to strategise the living area. I built floor to ceiling cupboards and painted them red and white. (Same red as the shed.) Behind those doors hide a multitude of sins. Well, actually no sins, really. Messy sins drive me frantic now, in a way they never did before the lymphoma. My small OCD problem, Steve calls it. OCD, ha! It's my proud German housekeeping finally showing its glorious nature. Order and structure, that's what makes life work. I wonder what the psychology is behind red. Anyway, he can scoff all he likes, but I know he actually applauds it.

Steve has taken over the little study as his retreat; not that he's ever home. I've moved my admin out into the shed. Now I have an organised spot for all the family storage inside. Camping stuff, old photos, books, the dress up box, toys, craft, etc, etc. I made a section in the middle of the shelves for all the cups and crockery and nice stuff. Stuff is such a good word. I've put glass doors on like I remember in my grandmother's house, with wooden panes. The television and sound system are in the middle. Very nice. The girls have a big drawer each, and one for Bump, so anything left lying around just gets thrown in their drawer and every Saturday morning they have to put it all away before sport. A bit tricky since the girls' games sometimes start at 7.30 a.m. now. Who plays sport at 7.30 in the morning?

November 1990

I have made a discovery! There's actually something glorious in chores. Who'd have guessed? Not me. Everything in its right place, just sitting there swinging its legs until it's used again, easily found, just where it should be. But it would be so good, so satisfying to have just one job a day that, once completed, wouldn't need to be repeated an hour later, or the next day, exactly as if it had never been done. I love ticking things off my list, but really, my household list is not fun. Bella and Katie are much more responsible now, mostly because I refuse to take them to their next activity until their own things are picked up and sorted.

I put on Bach as loudly as I could today – the girls thought I was mad – just for a change! Bach is so regulated and precise; I can feel my heart beat slow and count time. He always reminds me of a time when I knew it all and had my life at my feet; the uncomplicated life of someone who is loved, is young and lives at home. No responsibilities.

I've never been good at composing, I don't hear things like composers and arrangers do. I can hear it to know how to play it but I can't think up such glorious sounds, such combinations of sounds, such melody, harmony, cadence and symphony. Bella can. She already writes little songs on the piano.

Funny, though, for someone so obsessed with music, I don't miss being absorbed in it as much as I thought I would. Maybe I knew I'd never really make it; maybe that's why it was easy to go part-time when we got married. It made sense that one of us should work. Who knows? I'll encourage my girls to finish their careers before marrying.

So Steve is finally looking for houses with me. I think the thought truly crossed his mind that this pregnancy was all part of my evil plan to move into a bigger place!

We're spending a lot of time treading politely around each other over the issue. Now that business isn't so good for me, the houses and suburbs we might have been able to look at before are out of our reach. Which has a very good side, 'cause guess what? The only places we can afford are down south on the gorgeous Fleurieau Peninsula, into the hills – which could work because they're going to upgrade the freeway soon – or waaaaaaay out north, maybe even the Barossa. I could be bringing my children up in the beautiful Adelaide Hills after all. Shh. Don't cheer too loudly; Steve's a bit grumpy about it. Insert happy dance with one hand clasped on very round tummy and the other one over my mouth to shush the cheering.

December 1990

Mutti bought Peter Combe's Christmas CD, so we have modern songs as well as the lovely old carols. They're delightful! Destined to become part of Christmas tradition in our household. Bella has also been organising Christmas carols on the piano to give a family concert. Katie goes around to each person from Paddy to Opa, takes them by the hand and sings 'Merry Christmas to you, and to you and to you…' She has a surprisingly sweet voice (not a gift from me). Peter Combe would be so proud; well, maybe not if he could hear all the different keys his songs are sung in – all at the same time… They all have a part to play, I can't wait to see it.

Twelfth Night Party

What a fabulous party! The children invited friends and had to dress as their favourite fruit.

We invited friends and some Elie's Shed clients we've come to know. We asked everyone to bring a gift for Tear Fund. This is the night for gifts. Well, next Wednesday will be, but we celebrated tonight. I wanted the Christmas decorations to still be up. The Wise Men offered gifts so long ago and we had fun giving too. Everybody brought a plate of food and the house was aglow until well after midnight. We're going to have one every year.

10 February 1991

Ten weeks to go… Any time from now on – if the baby's ready – is fine with me. Really fine. I look like I swallowed a baby hippopotamus with gymnastic aspirations. Such an active baby. I hope this is just a temporary affliction – the temporarily active baby bit, I mean.

Previous trial experiments have already proven that the pregnancy has a finite time slot. Phew! Fancy coming back as an elephant! Can you imagine TWO WHOLE YEARS of this?

5 June 2011
To: Bella, Jack
<u>Subject: Hippos</u>

I understand the baby hippo analogy. My body is rebelling today. I think I'll go organise the pantry.

K and Bump-the-size-of-a-baby-hippo

6 June 2011
To: Katie, Jack
<u>Subject: Katie's in labour</u>

Who would have guessed the Wild Child has become a Mama? Very proper that we've gone from vegetable, mineral and finally to animal with this baby. I'm trusting it has one last metamorphosis!

I'm writing this as you go into hospital, Katie. Brad has promised to ring as soon as possible. I'm trying to keep busy with this scanning and Pa is with me at the Big House. Jack, where are you? I want you all around the fireplace tonight. I'll try ringing you again in a minute.

I'm watching Pa waiting to become a grandpa for the third time (of course, I was a little preoccupied the last two times to pay much attention). He's just so contained; he and Lachie are watching the sports channel on Fox as if it was a normal Saturday afternoon. Katie, your world is about to change forever.

I'm restless. What would Mama have been doing? Would she be out in her shed? No, she'd be sitting at the hospital, ready to step in and soothe away the pain and be the first to rejoice at the first cry. I'll do some more scanning, or go play the piano. My pantry's already organised.

Mmmm. Anyway, here's the next bit.

Love as always

Aunty Bella

<u>Attachment:</u>

March 1991

Baby's due in six weeks and no house yet. Business is looking good again – as Bella would say, timing, you suck!

7th

I've had to let all my clients know that all orders will now have a three-month wait. Have returned a few deposits and lost some clients, which is a shame now we are so established.

Thank goodness for Neville. He's going to keep on with enough jobs that he can manage. He's been so good to me.

I feel like that elephant: HUUUGE.

17 April

So, um, apparently we can make beautiful little boys too! 12 April, 4 p.m., 8lb exactly.

Charlotte has turned out to be a Jack. Which was a great surprise to us both, but not to Bella, who is not impressed with our choice of name. It's very difficult to get Steve's hands off him long enough to feed and let him sleep. When his daddy lets him go, both of his sisters want a hold. I feel a little superfluous. He's beautiful. Perfect. Looks just like his sisters but with dark eyes. Paddy's really pleased that at last there's another boy in the family. All that miserable sickness, fatigue and extra hundred kilograms were worth it. He's perfect.

Now, about moving.

22nd

I want to pack my bags and leave just like Bella did last year! I'm not convinced that Mummy's can't have tantrums as well. Steve has suggested that if I'm finding it too small here we could sell my stuff and extend into the shed!

Yes, I am finding it a bit cosy in here, but I want to work too! I love my tools and the wonderful moment when Neville and I stand back and admire the latest piece of furniture.

Why doesn't he want to move? Is there something going on I don't know about? Is work not going well? Has he met someone…? I want to curl up in a ball and cry myself to sleep. I think I might go out and do some sanding when the kids are asleep.

Steve has stayed at work for yet another meeting. We had this conversation on the phone. Again. Why do we have these horrid conversations on the phone and never face to face? When I challenged him about not wanting to come home, he asked me what he had to come home to? Aren't we enough? Not even cuddles with Jack keep him smiling for long.

I think my foundations are straining under the weight of this house too. Definite cracks.

25th

I can't move in this house! It's driving me nuts. Every weekend I go through the papers to find somewhere bigger that we can afford, and every weekend Steve gets grumpy and lists all the disadvantages of moving and the advantages for him of staying. At this point it'll be the kids and me moving and him staying. AAARRRGGGHHHH! Insert gripped fists, clenched teeth and sound of nerves snapping. Right now, that Jason recliner I used to dream of sitting in, the one next to Steve's, isn't even in the same house as his!

26th

Cracks have turned into fissures. No cave to hide in; even Chopin has turned his face away.

12 June 2011

To: Bella, Jack

<u>Subject: Such sadness</u>

Poor Mama and Pa. I never knew they were anything but happy together! When's the next instalment? Hospital is so boring!

They're kicking us out tomorrow for the Hilton Hotel! Can you believe it? Apparently it's cheaper for our insurance company than a private hospital and less nasty germs. No complaints from this little black duck.

Katie xoxo and sloppy kisses, milky burps and gurgles from Noah George; we won't mention the nappies.

12 June 2011
To: Katie, Jack
<u>Subject: Welcome to the story, Noah George!</u>

And what a handsome young man you are. Not like your cousins were at all, you've arrived in this world with a perfectly round head, beautiful skin and – like your cousins – a perfect pair of lungs. Katie, my love, next time you go into labour we'll suggest the midwife uses a catcher's mitt. Three hours from first to last push for a first baby is just scary.

I must say, Jack, it was really great that you left your friends to come to the hospital. When are we going to meet Claire? Is it still Claire? Or maybe Jane? Or was Jane the one before the one before…? No, that was Jessica :)

I was surprised, too, that our parents weren't always happy. So here it is, The First Story. I actually remember this one. We were waiting for Pa – again – and I had another ear infection. I lay across her lap with my ear against her breast. She smelt of baby cream and her voice was low and vibrated against my ear. Jack was one, so I must have been eleven. It was raining and cold and dark and we wanted to go home for tea. We were waiting in the car outside his work. I don't know why he was so late, and it was before mobile phones, so we were just waiting. Poor Mama indeed.

Love as always

Bella

<u>Attachment:</u>

April 1991

Steve's car is broken, so I've had to pack all the children up to collect him after work. This has gone on for two weeks and I hate peak-hour traffic with a passion. I don't care if Adelaide doesn't have a heavy peak hour in comparison with all the other capital cities he's been to, I HATE DRIVING THREE YOUNG CHILDREN AROUND IN IT! He's taking the train tomorrow.

Bella has another ear infection. So she was home from school again. Finally got her in to a specialist again and she's going to have more grommets put in her ears to see if we can get through a winter without any more infections.

Night-time routine took forever tonight. But I think everyone is happily asleep and I'm about to write my lists for tomorrow Remember how I said I was going to start writing the stories down? Well, a year later (drum roll…) here's tonight's story. I've included their interruptions 'cause I love it when they join in.

*

In A Time Long Ago and A Place Somewhere Else, there was a magnificent castle. In that castle lived a king and queen and their names were King Steven and Queen Elinor. Now King Steven and Queen Elinor had three beau-ti-ful children, and their names were Princess Bella, Princess Katie and Baby Prince Jack. One wet and rainy evening, Princess Bella, Princess Katie and Baby Prince Jack were sitting in a beautiful golden carriage waiting for King Steven to leave work.

'Was it wet and rainy, like this?' Katie asked, while she scribbled on some paper in the back seat.

'Oh, much wetter and much rainier than this!' I said. 'So wet and rainy, in fact, that the horses were wishing they'd brought their bathers!'

'Horses don't wear bathers!' Katie said, leaning back with her eyes almost closed, because she was very tired.

I wondered if she was going to suddenly nod off, or suddenly revive. You never can tell with Katie. 'Why not?' I asked, turning around, kissing Bella's head as I did. 'Maybe horses go swimming in the nude!' Here I covered my mouth with my hand as if I'd said a naughty word.

Katie giggled.

'What colour bathers do you think they'd have, Katie Jean?'

Katie didn't lift her head. She'd returned to her drawing, the tip of her little pink tongue just touching the side of her mouth. 'Purple bathers with stars all over them.'

'Very nice,' I agreed. 'So where were we…?' Ah, yes…

The horses were stamping their feet and complaining to each other about not having brought their bathers, when King Steven finally ran out of the palace offices and jumped into the carriage. Fortunately, the coachman knew that he would do this and managed to open the carriage door in time so King Steven didn't knock himself out.

'It's about time, Papa!' Princess Bella said, wiping the raindrops that he'd left on her face when he kissed her. 'We've been waiting for ever and a year for you and we're starving.'

If she was the foot-stamping kind of princess, she would have stamped her foot, but she wasn't, so she just frowned instead.

Princess Katie, however, was the foot-stamping kind of princess, so she jumped down off her seat and stamped her foot. 'Yes!' she agreed and tried to scramble back up onto the big leather seats, but she wasn't a very tall seven-year old and so King Steven had to help her.

'Well, I'm here now, so let's go home. Coachman!' he called out to the driver. 'Let's get these horses, I mean children, home!'

Well, you should have seen those horses take off. There's almost no traffic and it's very safe in A Place Somewhere Else, so the coachman let the horses run. And run they did! Straight through every puddle they could find. Puddles of mud and rainwater and grass and bits of all sorts of things came flying up against the coach sides, splashing the windows and making Baby Jack gurgle with laughter. Queen Elinor just held on tightly to Princess Bella, whose ears didn't like the swaying, while King Steven held the baby in one arm and Katie in the other.

'So what's for dinner tonight?' King Steven asked.

'You sound like the children,' Queen Elinor said. 'Well, we couldn't decide between fried snails and mud pies. We thought we'd leave it to you, didn't we, children?'

Princess Bella made choking noises and Princess Katie nodded until her curls tickled King Steven's nose so much he had to sneeze.

'Ker-CHOO!' he said.

'Oh, dear, I don't think we have any sneezes on the menu,' Queen Elinor said regretfully.

'But I don't want mud pies!' Katie started to say, when Princess Bella gave her a big 'it's a joke' wink. 'Oh,' she said, 'mud pies – and…ice cream.' She added the last bit and looked very pleased with herself.

By the time they got home, the fire was roaring in the family sitting room (they didn't use the big formal sitting room unless they had visitors). King Steven sat down and played with the children, while Queen Elinor took the dinner out of the oven.

It wasn't really mud pies and fried snails; only faeries eat that. They had spaghetti bolognese with cheese and pasta and absolutely-no-vegetables.

King Steven and Queen Elinor had bathed the children, helped them into their pyjamas, read them bedtime stories, sung them lullabies and kissed them goodnight; the children were already almost, but not quite, asleep.

'Mama,' Princess Bella said, 'my ear doesn't hurt any more.'

'That's the best goodnight news I've heard in a long time,' Queen Elinor said and bent to give them all butterfly kisses.

King Steven and Queen Elinor did the dishes since the servants had all gone home to their own families. They then cleared the kitchen and sat down to a quiet game of Scrabble in front of the fire, which King Steven always won because Queen Elinor wasn't a great speller.

And they all lived all the days of their lives.

20 June 2011

To: Katie, Jack

<u>Subject: My favourite story</u>

Here's some more for you both. She doesn't write much beyond calendars for a couple of years. I only have two young children and I haven't been sick but I still get tired. She must have been exhausted. Surprise, surprise. We weren't quiet little children. I don't remember us being particularly still either!

I have to say, occasionally I feel a bit uncomfortable reading her diaries. I don't like the idea of her not always being happy, or that she struggled quite badly sometimes. Katie, you found the right word. There's something in that last section that made her seem almost vulnerable. In my head she was always so tall and solid. Is that the right word? Solid? Even when she first got sick. Maybe that's because she was the same height as Papa and she had that open face, wide smile and she didn't grow old enough for wrinkles.

Anyway, here's the next bit.

Bella

<u>Attachment:</u>

February 1994

Jack has turned into a fearless tike. I think he'll grow up to be a bulldozer or maybe an SAS specialist: he has this habit of jumping out at people from behind doors and from on top of furniture. A bit Cato-like, actually; his mission is to annihilate all dragons and lions. These, unfortunately, often take the shape of his sisters, most particularly Katie; even she doesn't have the stamina of her brother (how did I manage to produce such a fine-boned elf?). I think what he needs is a gang of mates to take all his energy out on. But he gives me the most delicious cuddles. Sometimes he spends ages climbing on my back as I go about the day. It's like having a baby koala on my back. I am Mama Bear…

I'm beyond exhausted. Jack refuses to take naps in the afternoon now, so I've brought back the old 'go to the hairdressers' trick. When I was ill, I'd go to the hairdressers every afternoon around 2 p.m. This would mean I used to lie down with my head at the end of my bed, while Katie and Bella were armed with every hair tie they could find and a couple of hairbrushes. I'd divide my hair into two halves and close my eyes for sometimes up to forty minutes. Scissors were strictly banned. But even twenty minutes can be so sweet. Such bliss!

So I thought I'd try it with Jack. You know, one of those science experiment type things… I should have videoed it! The result, of course, was nothing short of gothic, and I had to convince Jack that jumping up and down on the bed was not the way to style someone's hair. He didn't really seem to get the point.

*

In A Time Long Ago and A Place Somewhere Else, there was a magnificent castle. In that castle lived a king and queen and their names were King Steven and Queen Elinor. Now King Steven and Queen Elinor had three beau-ti-ful children, and their names were Princess Bella, Princess Katie and Young Prince Jack.

Queen Elinor was lying down – again – and it was time for all good royal families to have a rest. Prince Jack and Mollydog were busy experimenting with the idea that the faster you run, the less you bump into things. So far, the experiment wasn't working very well.

Princesses Bella and Katie were at school.

Queen Elinor was tired again and she had an important dinner to go to that night, so she asked them both if they'd like to help her decide on a hairstyle. They both agreed at once and Jack went off to find some scissors. When he returned, Mollydog also returned with two hairbrushes and all the bobby pins and hair bands and ribbons and hair clips ever owned by the family.

'Right!' Jack said, jumping on to the bed like a man on a mission. 'I'll start with your fringe.'

It was only then that Queen Elinor noticed the scissors in his hand

and the purposeful way he was waving them around. 'Wait!' she cried, sitting up in an awful hurry. 'Just what were you going to do with those?'

Prince Jack was delighted with the question and his smile lit up his little face and his dark eyes twinkled dangerously. 'Oh, these? I was going to give you a beautiful cut and style, just like you said.'

Mollydog was miffed that she hadn't thought of that and was just about to go and find a pair for herself when Queen Elinor put an end to the idea altogether.

'Well, that is very thoughtful of you, but actually we're not supposed to cut hair unless we have a special hair-cutting licence, and that needs years of training, lots of discipline, working hard for not very much pay, with customers who don't like what you've done and want their money back, sometimes even little boys and girls – and puppies - who don't want their hair cut at all and try and bite your scissors in half before you've even started. But if you want to learn, I can ask the royal hairdresser to have you work for him.'

They both thought better of the idea and Jack put his scissors away before coming back to fix his mother's hair.

In no time at all, Mollydog and Prince Jack were having so much fun. There were ribbons here and ribbons there and clips just about everywhere. It was a good thing that Queen Elinor had so much hair.

'How much hair did she have?' Jack asked.

'I don't know,' I said. 'How much do you think she should have?'

'As much as Rapunzel,' Katie suggested.

'Yeah!' Jack's face lit up. 'Then they could climb to the top of the tower and throw the plait down and swing from it!'

'Ouch!' I said. 'That would hurt, wouldn't it? What if they just thought she had lots of hair but she didn't really?'

'No.' Katie shook her head. 'That wouldn't do at all. They'd notice if she didn't really have that much hair. I think it should be just this much hair.' And she held up my shoulder-length mess and continued brushing it.

Okay, back to our story…

So it was a good thing that Queen Elinor had enough hair to go around. The two worked hard for ages, maybe even fifteen minutes. It was then that Prince Jack began to get jumpy. I mean really jumpy. He leapt onto the bed where his mother was trying to lie still with her head just over the edge and her hair falling over the edge…

'You lie down a lot, don't you, Mama?' Katie interrupted me.

Bella looked at me; her eyes go cloudy when she's worried.

'Yes, I guess I do. So, back to Prince Jack…'

At that moment, Mollydog, who had got bored very quickly and left, came back into the room to check on things and to ask for food. She took one look at Jack and decided that some intervention was needed. Jumping up onto the bed, she tickled his ear and the backs of his knees and then jumped off with a bark and a wag of her tail. Prince Jack took the challenge and raced out after her.

When King Steven returned that evening, he noticed how beautiful his wife was looking and immediately decided to have Mollydog look after the children, told Queen Elinor to change into some Cinderella clothes and swept her out for a dinner at Windy Point Restaurant. Her hair was beautiful and everyone they passed smiled and commented on it and King Steven looked very proud.

'It didn't really happen that way.' Jack looked at his sisters a little embarrassed.

'No. Mollydog was the one who did her hair.'

4 July 2011

To: Bella, Katie

<u>Subject: Slimy nappies</u>

Dear Noah

I'm delighted to read that you are continuing the time-honoured tradition, started by yours truly, of grossing your mother out with the wonder that is the male bowel. Nice work, son. I pledge you my solemn oath that I will undertake to train you in the finer art of farting. Ever your mother's favourite.

In appreciation,

Your Uncle Jack

4 July 2011

To: Bella, Jack

<u>Re: Slimy nappies</u>

Dear Uncle Jack

My mama has started stocking up on Blu-tack. She says that wine corks are hard to find these days.

Should I be worried?

Yours in trepidation

Your fragile, baby nephew, Noah George

4 July 2011

To: Bella, Katie

<u>Re: Slimy nappies</u>

Dear Noah

Nah. She's bluffin'. I've got your back, mate.

In appreciation,

Uncle Jack

8 July 2011

To: Katie, Jack

<u>Subject: Opa and Oma to the rescue again!</u>

And my one and only rebellion. Poor Katie. But even you, Noah, darling, could not rival the wonder of human anatomy that is Uncle Jack's bowel.

This bit of diary's not so light-hearted. I don't know about you, but I don't like the idea of our parents falling out of love. I don't like the idea that maybe there was a time when they weren't such good friends. I guess I idealised them that way. It made it more comfortable for me. But of course, they must have had bumps. Pa always over-engineers each decision or plan and Mama would just go and do it. And then, of course, when the roles reversed at the end, they were inseparable.

BTW, if anyone's in town this weekend, family tea will be outside, so bring coats. I found chestnuts at Central Market! I'm having chestnut roasting outside in the brazier, some nice wine, maybe mulled, soup, fresh bread…

Love as always

Bella

<u>Attachment:</u>

April 1994

My parents have made an intervention. Last week, after Mutti had been round, and Papa had joined us for tea, we put the children to bed and they gave us the talk.

I had no idea how consumed with my own life I'd become. Apparently, Papa has been keeping an eye on Steve lately and, fortunately, Steve has had someone (male) to talk with. Who would have thought small children and a successful business could take so much of my time! Steve was feeling like an afterthought. Apparently he felt shut out of the shed, and Neville used to be his friend and now they hardly see each other without me. He's going to come home more often.

So we have to develop some golden time, Mutti calls it. We've let our monthly dates go; I can't even remember the last time we had one. And how we actually got pregnant with Jack is a bit of a mystery. So once a month again, they'll have ALL the children over night. All three! I have the best parents.

They asked me when the last time was that I played the piano. Do we even have one still? I think it's been hiding in its corner waiting to be noticed. We don't sing round the piano any more. Bella plays occasionally; I found her playing nursery rhymes with Jack on her lap the other day and had a sudden flashback of me with her on my lap. I think we got lost somewhere – I got lost somewhere.

So, date nights are happening – not fancy dinners out, but definitely out of the house. It took only three dates before we stopped arguing or bringing up 'why did you...' or 'but you always/never...'

The kids don't spend as much time on the trampoline any more.

14th

Bella dyed her beautiful long hair red. My placid, sensible girl. Not auburn, not chestnut, but my-shed-door-red! She looks like BoBo the Clown's daughter! If this is rebellion, I can take it.

12 July 2011

To: Katie, Jack

<u>Subject: Enter the BIG HOUSE</u>

Hey,

Sorry I haven't written for ages. That was a fun night we had around the chestnuts. Pa loved having everyone around and I've attached some photos. There's a great one of him holding little Noah, who looks so like his dad, and Madi and Jackson leaning over his shoulder laughing. Even Pa is smiling. You can just see Opa walking past in the background. I'm going to print and frame that one.

Katie, what do you think of our little brother giving up a stunning, if nomadic, career as an accountant to become a carpenter? No real surprise there. I like the idea of you buying into Opa's business, Jack.

But that was always the plan, wasn't it? Are you going to work part-time? Start an apprenticeship all over again? And what will you do with your accounting degree? You'll have to stop all that jet-setting.

Or could it be you may be thinking of settling for bit? How great to have one of us follow in the family business! You can create your own Red Door. You know there's a shed here; the doors may need repainting – I have it on the highest authority (mine) that they used to be this vibrant red colour – just waiting to be used for a workshop...

Anyway. Back to business. Do you remember the autumn after we moved in here to the Big House? The tramping every weekend through the grey, wet days trying to find a bigger house? One that would fit us all in? We'd come home to hot soup, or toasty-toasties with cheese and ham and hot chocolates and stories. Even Pa would sit and listen. Mama would turn the lights off and leave just the flames of the combustion heater in that tiny little family room. She would sit and read, but the best stories were hers.

What do you remember about the move? We were all so excited; we were going to share four bedrooms instead of two! The house was enormous and because we only had furniture enough for our little house, some of the rooms were empty and almost empty and we could race around and play hide and seek inside and set up commando courses in the playroom. It was no wonder we had so many accidents. How was Mama not grey before her time? I heard her telling someone once that she was considering stapling mattresses to the walls and floors. I wonder if it would have helped.

Here's some more diary. Sorry I've been so slow.

Love as always

<u>Attachment:</u>

May 1994

We've found it! Actually, Steve found it! Which is extra exciting. A property on top of Chandlers Hill. It'll take Steve no more than forty minutes straight down South Road to work if he leaves early enough. He says this will work well because it'll mean he can leave work earlier at the end of the day. He's been much better about coming home in the evenings this last year, so this is really good for all of us. For me.

Huge homestead with an orchard and what used to be a vegie patch. Wooden floors and open fireplaces. Yes! And even better, a bedroom for everyone. And for me, *la pièce de resistance*! Three huge, I mean HUGE sheds, so I'll paint the doors of one of them with bright fire engine red paint and get out my tools...

However, it will mean that Mutti can only come once a fortnight now, but I'll only have young Jack at home, so it should be okay (fingers toes and all however-many-there-are-kms of intestines crossed that it is so!). Neville's pleased because he and Jean live at Willunga, which is only thirty minutes' drive away. Win win win, I say.

The girls can have a pony and Steve is going to make a BMX track for them all. Mollydog can roam free to her heart's content. How do girls manage to be princesses and Evel Knievel all at the same time? Settlement is in sixty days.

July 1994

The great thing about taking on a bigger home loan is that you can hide little costs like a professional removalist to move you. This is quite a big task for us because of all my gear.

But I am going to open up Elie's Shed again.

The story tonight was about the family picking up the castle and transporting it straddled on a million trillion boats across the water across the sea into a new land, much bigger, much more magical. Mollydog took the helm in the front boat, like a pilot ship, to make sure that none of the little boats got confused and headed in the wrong direction. It was a happy story.

I am surprised, though. Packing up and leaving has been like chopping a leg off. The children are all excited about the move and the bigger house and the possibilities, but this is all they've known; this is, for the girls, their whole childhood. This was our marriage until now. Our family until now. Have I done the right thing? Insisting on this move, all that complaining. Was I just wishing for what I didn't have instead of loving what I did? Are we doing the right thing to leave our little house?

I had to leave my beloved red doors behind, but we've dismantled the tree house. It was too cold to sleep on the trampoline, but we lit the brazier and roasted marshmallows.

Steve and I opened a bottle of champagne and the children had some fizzy drinks. Our last night.

30th

I'm going to open Elie's Shed again soon. Tomorrow.

August 1994

Tomorrow.

9th

So Neville came up and he and Steve, Paddy, Papa and I set the shed up. It already had power, so we just had to have half of it clad to protect the wooden furniture and to create an office space for me. I'm going to paint the shed doors fire engine red again. Elie's Shed is going to undergo a transformation, just like Elie did. It will be the Red Door Furniture and More. Red Door. Something strong and vibrant in that, don't you think?

Anyway, Steve and I have an arrangement. That I won't work more than three days a week until young Jack is in grade 2 or 3. I realise that I have the capacity to lose myself in my loves. There'll be time later to become a multinational corporation with workshops all over the planet. Later, when the children have grown and moved away. Neville's going to help me those three days and he'll work as many after that as he wants to. We're going to go back to what we were good at in the beginning, which is restoring old stuff before creating our own. This will keep our product boutique and hopefully special enough.

The children are delighted with everything. The property's huge and we have no intention of farming it ourselves. We'll just let it revert to bush. It'll be difficult enough to manage the orchard and vegetables. But I will have chickens and we will make a track for their bikes. Time enough for ponies.

We want to make the house a place where even the girls' school friends will want to come up and visit. Why is it that people who live on the plains think they have to pack a picnic and sleeping bag to drive twenty minutes into the hills, but won't even blink travelling that distance in the other direction?

*

In A Time Long Ago and A Place Somewhere Else, there was a magnificent castle. In that castle, lived King Steven and Queen Elinor and their three beau-ti-ful children. They were called Princess Bella, Princess Katie, Prince Jack and, of course, Queen Molly the Dog…

'I don't want to be Prince Jack!' Jack yelled from somewhere under my feet.

I'd thought he wasn't listening, since his head was stuck under the bed and all that could be seen of him was from his knees down. I yanked the sock from his left foot. 'Why's that, boy?' I asked.

'Prince Jack is a stupid name. I want to be King Jack, or a Sir Jack and catch dragons and tie them up, or a Captain Jack,' he replied in a serious little voice that sounded as if he had a couple of fingers in his mouth. 'I don't want to be a prince.'

'Okay! Of course you wouldn't. That makes much more sense, because there could be lots of dragons in a big place like Somewhere Else. What about Captain Jack, then?'

There was silence from under the bed, which I took to be an agreement. 'So where were we? Ah yes, Prince Jack and, of course, Queen Molly –'

'Captain!'

'Captain Jack, of course, and Queen Molly –'

'Can a puppy be a queen?' Katie asked, scratching Mollydog's ears.

'Well, she's not much of a puppy any more and puppies can be anything I want them to be, in my Place Somewhere Else,' I declared. 'Now snuggle in and listen…'

One fine day, the children decided to set off for a picnic in the woods – well, the scrub. They knew the woods, I mean scrub, very well because they played in there all the time with their parents, when their parents weren't busy being king and queen of Somewhere Else. In fact, their father, King Steven, had had some tree houses made in the largest of the oak trees.

'You don't mind if I put oak trees in the scrub, do you? I'm very partial to oak trees. No? Thank you.'

They could spend hours in there, playing hide and seek or pretending to hunt dragons, or capture Unsuspecting Grown-ups who had mistaken their wood for a nice place to paint, or walk or hunt rabbits. Today they hadn't decided yet what they would do, but were fairly certain they would know when they found it.

Princess Bella, being the eldest, decided it was her turn to choose the picnic place. It had been Queen Mollydog's turn really, but the older children thought she was a little too prone to racing off to chase rabbits at inconvenient moments to make important decisions like that. The children gathered solemnly in the kitchen, ten minutes before they wanted to leave. (It's always good to do this, so that you can double check that you have everything ready for your expedition.)

'I have all the safety gear. Katie. Do you have all the camping gear?'

'Yes, but I still don't understand why we need to take tents if we're just going on a picnic,' she grumbled. 'I had a lot of trouble dragging these out of the second tower and down the staircase. Someone left one of Mollydog's balls on the stairs and I slid on it.'

'Poor Katie,' Princess Bella said with a sympathetic smile. 'But you have them. Jack, do you have the dragon-capturing kit?'

'Yes, I do!' he answered, holding up his backpack filled with an old sheet and some shoelaces – gathered from the shoe rack by the back door – and some official-looking plastic handcuffs which he'd been given for his birthday the year before.

'Excellent then, Mollydog can pull the picnic basket. Let's go!'

With that, Princess Bella placed whistles around everyone's necks – in case they got lost, so they could whistle for help – picked up the map-making stuff and some pencils and headed out the door with everyone following behind.

'Wait!' Queen Elinor called from the kitchen. 'You haven't kissed me goodbye and you haven't left me a map of where you're going.'

The children all hurried back in to give their mother a kiss and Princess Bella kindly explained that they hadn't left a map because they hadn't drawn it yet. They had to then promise that they wouldn't go so far that they couldn't see the castle.

It was a lovely morning for a picnic. The children and Queen Mollydog were very excited. They talked about all the monsters and dragons they might bump into and have to arrest, or the helpless stray train engines that Captain Jack thought might have misplaced their tracks and got lost.

They travelled for a long, long time, maybe even five minutes, when Princess Bella suddenly stopped. 'Stop! Shush!' she said in a loud sort of whisper and held up a hand.

The children all stopped, except Queen Mollydog, who had found an interesting scent and had to be called back.

'What is it, Bella?' Princess Katie asked, tilting her head to one side so that her honey-coloured curls bounced over her shoulder.

'We-ell,' her big sister continued slowly, 'it might be a dragon, or it might just be a sleep-walking wombat, or it might be Something Else altogether...' she finished in a mysterious voice.

'While we're stopped,' began Captain Jack, 'can we eat the picnic?'

Princess Katie reached into the basket which the amazing Queen Mollydog had dragged all this time and pulled out an apple. 'An apple? Yuck!' he said with disgust.

'Aha – but it could be the magic apple,' Katie told him with a big-sister smile at Princess Bella.

'Really? A really magic one?' he asked. 'How will I know?'

'Well, I think you have to eat it all up and if the core's made of gold, you know you've found the magic one,' she explained. 'But if you don't want it, I'll eat it.'

'No, no!' Captain Jack said, backing out of arm's reach. 'I'll just eat and see.'

'Right. Back to that sound: what do you think we should do?' Princess Bella asked them all, her hands on her hips now.

I stopped and looked at the faces watching me. 'So what do you think they might have found? It might have been an elephant…' I suggested in a hopeful sort of voice.

'Well, maybe,' said Bella, kindly, 'but I don't think that there are many elephants in the Australian scrub.'

'It was probably just an insomniac wombat,' Katie suggested.

'What's insomniac mean?' Jack asked.

'That's someone who can't sleep when they're s'posed to,' Bella said. 'Actually, I think it could have been an elephant,' she went on, warming up to the idea. 'A great big grey one like we saw on TV – you know, about Thailand. The one which was as big as a house, with a bright red rug on its back.'

'Yes!' Katie clapped her hands in excitement. 'A red rug with gold tassels!'

'Okay, but the elephant may have to be smaller than that,' I said. 'Now let's see…ah, yes…'

So, just as Princess Bella finished asking them all what should be done, a long grey trunk came snaking out from behind a tree and slurped up the apple from Captain Jack's hands.

'Oi!' Captain Jack cried. 'I was eating that! Bella, an elephant just stole my magic apple!'

Princess Bella laughed aloud. 'Yes, and now we'll never know if it was magic or not. Maybe you'd better eat another one.'

'What will happen to the elephant if he eats my apple and it really was the magic one?' Captain Jack asked.

They all turned to Princess Bella, except for Queen Mollydog, who was busy trying to pull the picnic basket and chase her own tail.

Bella put her head on one side, which is what she did when she was thinking. 'I don't know,' she said finally. 'Let's find out.' And with that she pushed apart the bushes where the elephant's trunk had been and, sure enough, there was a teeny wee baby elephant still munching happily on Captain Jack's apple.

The elephant looked at the children and blinked and the children looked back at the elephant, hopefully. They'd never seen an elephant in the bush before and they were hoping that the apple really had been magic and something astonishing was about to happen.

So the elephant and the children stared at each other for – oh, for ages – until Captain Jack squared his shoulders and put his fists to his hips.

'That can't have been the magic apple, Katie,' he said.

Princess Katie smiled her twinkly smile. 'But don't you think it's a bit magical that there is an elephant here at all? I think that is very odd.'

'Yes,' agreed Princess Bella. 'Let's see if he wants to come on the picnic with us.'

To the children's surprise, the elephant said that he'd be delighted to join them on the picnic and were there going to be any more apples like the one he had just eaten?

'Elephants don't talk,' Bella mentioned quietly.

'Shhhh!' the others said.

'This is in A Place Somewhere Else. Elephants can talk if they want to. But you have to be a very nice sort of a person for them to speak to you,' I explained.

Bella sighed heavily and shook her head in a patient way. 'All right, so the elephant talks.'

'Yes. So where were we...'

Captain Jack was so impressed with having a talking elephant that he completely forgot about the apple.

Princess Bella decided that they'd better set up the picnic ground where they were since they'd wasted so much time. The children set about clearing the ground and putting all their packages and bags down in separate places, while Bella unpacked the picnic basket. There were hardboiled eggs, cucumber slices, cupcakes, chocolate-chip cookies, fritz and sauce sandwiches and, best of all, Queen Elinor's favourite chocolate cake covered in coloured sprinkles.

Princess Bella passed around the paper plates and poured the home-made lemon cordial before passing round the cups. They all looked about them and were about to begin eating when the elephant gave a snort of delight and sucked up the small bowl of apples.

The children all looked shocked and Captain Jack stuck up one chubby little finger and said, 'No, no, no!' in a growly voice that sounded very much like Queen Elinor when she was telling them off.

The elephant looked very embarrassed. 'I'm terribly sorry,' he said. 'Did I do something wrong?'

'Yes,' Bella nodded. 'It's bad manners to snatch. Now none of us can have an apple because you've gobbled them all.'

The poor baby elephant dropped his trunk to the ground and lowered his long lashes over his eyes. 'I'm very sorry. I didn't know.'

'Well, now you do,' Bella said. 'Katie, please pass round the sandwiches. Baby elephant is a guest so offer him one first.'

I think Baby Elephant wasn't expecting to be included in the meal since he had disgraced himself, so he glanced quickly at all the children and then very carefully selected the sandwich nearest to him on the plate.

Jack was busy trying to climb on Mollydog's back while this was going on, until he spied the chocolate cake. 'Shotgun!' he cried in delight.

Princess Bella just managed to scoop the cake away as her brother made a dive off Queen Mollydog's back and onto the picnic rug, narrowly missing the cordial jug, but not missing Princess Katie's back.

Katie had been busy munching her fritz sandwich while chasing an ant with a finger sticky with sauce. 'Oompf,' she said as she rolled her little brother off her back and continued the chase.

'That,' said Princess Bella to Baby Elephant, 'is also bad manners, but he's still learning, like you.'

Baby Elephant looked a little wistful at that. 'You mean,' he said, 'that it isn't good manners to dive onto your food?'

Captain Jack shook his head sadly. 'No, it's very bad manners. Here, have some cookies. We made them.'

Captain Jack, Baby Elephant and Queen Molly were busy finishing off the remains of their plates as the older children packed the picnic away.

Jack climbed onto my lap. 'Mama, what happens to little boys, if his mummy isn't there when he gets home?' He snuggled into my chest.

'Why, she makes sure that there's always someone for him to come home to instead.' I was surprised he should even have thought that. 'Why?'

'I just think about that sometimes. What if she never comes home again?' he persisted.

What a terrifying thought! I squeezed him veeery tightly. 'She squeezes him like this – a lot – when she is home so he never forgets how much she loves being with him and if she could that's where she'd always be. Always.'

He seemed satisfied with that.

'I think it's time to go home,' Princess Bella added. 'Mama has raised the yellow flag, which means it's time for tea. Would you like to come home with us, Baby Elephant?'

'Oh, yes please,' Baby Elephant said and gave a funny little skip. Actually, it was a very funny skip, because elephants aren't very graceful dancers. 'I'll carry the picnic basket if you like.'

'Bella,' Captain Jack tugged on her T-shirt, 'what happens to little boys if their mothers aren't home when they get there?'

His sister shrugged. 'Well, they make sure that someone else is. Always. Do you want to ride on Baby Elephant?'

Baby Elephant picked him up very gently and put him on his back, picked up the picnic basket and the camping gear, then turned to follow the older children back to the castle.

Jack swayed from his high perch and sang, 'Haydee, haydee-ho, the great big elephant is so slow…'

Katie hopped on one leg most of the way just for fun, until a thought occurred to her. 'Hey, Bella!' she whispered. 'I bet you Pa lets us keep him.'

Then she ran up to Queen Mollydog, tagged her tail and ran off as fast as she could. Mollydog tried to catch up.

'Magic,' said Princess Bella to Baby Elephant, 'is what happens when we make new friends unexpectedly, I think.'

And they all made their way back to the castle, where Queen Elinor lifted Captain Jack off Baby Elephant's back. She'd had a lovely time in her shed while they were playing.

'Thank you, Baby Elephant. Here's King Steven. I expect the children will want to keep you, so I'll see you when I come back downstairs.'

19 July 2011
To: Katie, Jack
<u>Subject:</u>

Katie, no one would have guessed you'd grow into such a tall and elegant woman! You couldn't catch a ball until you were just about through high school, when you grew three metres and filled out in all the right places.

So here's some more – not so happy, poor Mama. Sometimes, I think that Once Upon a Time begins the worst kind of nightmares known to mankind. These are the ones that end up, 'and they all lived happily ever after'. But you know and I know that that isn't how the story really goes. Princes and princesses – and knights – are the very best of us, while wicked witches and dragons the very worst.

What really happens is the mess and tragedy of everyday life with laughter and loving in between. I've thought long and hard about how sad the awakening can be. Not Sleeping Beauty's awakening to True Love's kiss; no, I mean the awakening to the fact that love is never enough to stop bad things happening; sometimes all that's left of the fairy tale is the outside cover, maybe a little tattered from lots of use, maybe with a few pages left, torn or perhaps coffee stains on some and teardrops on others. Perhaps it's what it represents that holds the real magic. What it used to mean. I don't know any more. Mama knew it too, and that's why she never used that line.

But here we are, another year on, creating traditions of our own. We have us and our own families with all our faults and traumas – and don't you think it's funny that we all want trampolines in our backyards? The more I read, the sadder I am. Did any of us really know her? Did you know how sad or tired or alone she felt? I remember her being grumpy sometimes, but even when she started lying down a lot, she'd always give us her attention and laugh with us.

Katie, you were talking about her getting grumpy and how great it was to have the trampoline as 'barleys'. Having had children of my own, I understand now why she got cranky sometimes. What did she call it? 'Throwing wobblies'? Was that it? I remember one of those times. I always thought it was in the old house, but finding it here, it must have been soon after we moved into the big house. We'd all been making pancakes in the kitchen and hadn't cleaned up. She'd been yelling at us and she was so loud and scary. We all scattered in different directions. The next day she sat down and read us a story she'd written the night before. Well, there's a copy of that here too.

Love as always

Bella

<u>Attachment:</u>

December 1994

The new house is still so big. I find myself rearranging the furniture into little corners and walking into cupboards thinking they're doorways. The big children have set up a scooter circuit around the pantry and passageway, around and around and around. I'm always anxious that Jack will get bowled over by the girls, but then I have to let go and let them all have fun. Bella or Katie will sometimes take him onto their scooters with them as they race That doesn't make me feel any calmer. I think my children are going to grow up to enjoy extreme sports or take up careers as pyro-technicians or high school teachers. High adrenalin.

Moving house is sooo complicated. Steve and I have been arguing again and the kids have made a secret pact to leave as much stuff around the house and boycott all jobs. I'm so grateful they have the trampoline, because sometimes I think that without it there'd be a lot more grumpy-mummy by now. Thank God their father has been coming home early still.

I appreciate the backup, but I wish it wouldn't get so desperate in the first place. What happened to white picket fences, banksia roses, Brady Bunch dynamics, and other fairy tale endings? Katie told the story tonight while I lay down on Bella's bed with Jack and tried to keep breathing. I wrote a story for myself tonight on the computer, but I'm not going to read it to them. It's for me, I think.

Katie slumped down on the back steps. I watched her through the open French doors as she dropped her chin in her hands and tried hard not to cry.

'It's not fair!' she grumbled. 'Mama's allowed to have tantrums but we aren't!'

Jack threw a stone and dropped down beside her and continued to throw stones from the stash in his pocket across the lawn. He was mumbling all the rude words he could think of under his breath as he threw each one. He was really mad.

Inside, they could hear their mother's voice yelling at Bella.

'Yep,' Katie said, 'she's really throwing a tantrum.'

They could hear Bella yelling back and then come storming out the back door. Katie and Jack made room on the step for her to sit down.

Mollydog peeked her head around the corner of the house.

Katie looked up for a minute. 'You in trouble too?' she asked.

Mollydog shook her head and wagged her tail as if to say, 'I'm keeping OUT of trouble. She's really mad today!'

'How come grown-ups can throw tantrums and get away with it?' Katie asked.

'We-e-ll,' Bella said, taking a deep breath to calm her own temper, 'it's like this. Sometimes we get so grumpy inside that we explode. Mama says that being little is when we learn what to do when we feel that bad. That's what being a kid is all about. Learning. Sometimes when you're a grown-up, you forget. We think it's REALLY bad, 'cause it doesn't happen as often for them as it does for us.'

'Yeah,' Katie added, 'but when it does, it really, really does. Uh-oh!' She stopped. 'Here she comes!'

They heard their mother's footsteps, and then she opened the door. She'd been crying too. She had a box of tissues in her hand. 'Hi, guys,' she said.

They didn't say anything. Jack threw three stones all at once.

'I'm sorry. I just threw a wobbly and I acted badly and I yelled at you for stuff that didn't need yelling about.'

They still didn't say anything.

Katie folded her arms, 'You yelled at us for not tidying up and for shouting too loud and for fighting with each other and throwing tantrums. We did tidy a bit, but you were just lying down again and then YOU threw a worse one. And you leave stuff lying around and you fight with Pa sometimes, and YOU are s'posed to be the grown-up, and WE get the punishment.'

'Well,' Mama said, 'you're right. I'm not allowed to talk to you like that. It's my job to tell you when you're not behaving properly and to make sure you behave the right way. So I need to tell you off, but I was wrong to let my anger explode. I hurt you guys a lot and I'm sorry because you mean so much to me, each of you.'

Bella came and kissed her cheek. 'That's okay,' she said.

'No, it's not!' shouted Katie and Jack.

'She doesn't get into trouble!' Katie added.

'No, I don't.' Mama grinned. 'That's one of the good things about being a grown-up. But your father will tell me off when he comes home. You can tell him all about it then, and I promise that you can tell him first,' she added.

'Can I tell him you yelled till my ears hurt?' asked Jack.

'Yep,' said Mama, plopping down on the step, feeling suddenly very tired again.

'I'm going to tell him that you told us we were bad children!' Bella said.

'Mmmn, that was wrong of me. We DO bad things but we're not bad people. You're quite right to be cross with me for that. I'm sorry.'

'And you took away my videos for ever!' added Katie.

'That wasn't really fair, because nobody does naughty things for ever. We'll make that much shorter, maybe for just the rest of today. But you still have to tidy up all the kitchen mess you made.'

They all sat for a while watching Mollydog pretend to be a great hunter on the back lawn. She was trying to creep up on a magpie.

'Whose turn is it to choose afternoon tea?' their mother asked as she stood up to go inside.

'It might be mine,' said Katie as she aimed little kicks at the top stair. 'But that doesn't mean I'm not mad at you any more.'

Their mother smiled, 'Of course, it doesn't. Just like it doesn't mean you guys can leave all your mess lying around, but it does mean I can't throw tantrums about it. And it doesn't change the fact that I love you.'

24 July 2011

To: Katie, Jack

<u>Subject: Another time lapse/Christmas in July</u>

Hi All,

Winter wraps around us again and I find myself remembering lots more. She loved cold weather, didn't she? We always loved the summer. She loved cold evenings and would light a fire for any reason and we'd wrap our fingers around mugs of soup while she told or read us stories. She had traditions of winters we found it hard to even guess at. All that European history that spoke of generations of European Christmases, frosty red noses and chilled fingers, the taste of snow in the air before the snow clouds blanketed the sky. The sound of the slush of cars in the street as the wheels turned the pretty white snow to dirty grey.

I'm sure this was her battle with Christmas. In her head, she had memories of children's noses pressed to shop windows. Windows that would be rich and sparkling with red and green and gold decorations, tiny little handcrafted wonders for real fir trees. Green and red coffee stands filled with people wrapped and bundled in thick winter coats and stylish hats and scarves, stomping their feet while they chatted to each other, their breath condensing round their faces.

She'd say, 'There's something missing here,' as we added buckets of water to the Christmas tree every day to keep it from dropping its needles everywhere.

I remember the baking day. It was compulsory to like gingerbread biscuits even though we didn't really like them. She'd bake our great-great-great grandmother's gingerbread recipe every November. It was a family affair. She'd stand us all around the table with the ingredients laid out and everyone would have a job to do. We all had an ingredient to measure and add and we all had a bowl with a wooden spoon. She managed to find, from somewhere, child-sized rolling pins so we each had one. And so the production line would begin. It took every one of us a few gingerbread-baking days to realise that the delicious biscuit dough was best left uneaten. I think that's why we actually never really liked the baked biscuits; our tummies would be full and sick with the memory of sneaking too much dough.

There'd always be tins of it, though. Not the dough, the biscuits Some of them would be iced by our own fair hands and the others she would turn into kookaburras and gingerbread men and women with bright-coloured clothes with sultana faces. For some reason, the kookaburras always tasted the best. There'd be tins full for everyone for morning or afternoon teatime and they tasted so good dipped in glasses of milk. Cold milk.

Every Christmas we would go around to Opa and Oma's for the ceremonial nativity scene to help put it all together. This was one of Mama's favourite rituals and another one we never really enjoyed as much as she did. I don't know why. I remember the year Opa waited all day for us to come around to help and Mama was so tired she just forgot. He waited until evening and when he rang, she cried – no noise, just big tears rolling don her face.

It was the beginning of different Christmases for us. The more she struggled, the more disappointing it was for all of us.

Love as always

Bella

Attachment:____

December 1996

I can't believe it's nearly Christmas again. I hate Christmas now. I hate the disappointment in their eyes every morning. I hate that I cannot seem to organise my way to something special for them. I used to be so organised! I used to love this whole thing. They were happy with the little things we could provide and I'd be all ready and relaxed weeks ahead. I'd play carols and dress the tree. I feel like I'm in this all by myself. I shop for the presents by myself or I dress the tree by myself, and all of it in this horrible grey semi-coma I live in.

Sometimes it feels like my body is fighting itself and I wake up hurting everywhere and like my limbs are dead weights I must lug around for another day, while everyone else dances. My little elves dance their way through the day and I've forgotten the steps. I worry at the back of my mind if this is lymphoma all over again, but truly there's so much going on. I think I'm just over-tired.

Tonight it's carols night again at the school. This will be the first year that Jack will be in it and we used to love this night so much. Where did all that time go? Did I even mention that Bella's in secondary school now? What has happened to me? The children will do their items class by class; all the families will sit on the oval on blankets and chairs and open their picnic tea. I'll spend the evening trying to stop Jack from lighting everybody's lanterns or surprising them with a stacks-on assault from behind. I'll watch all the couples enjoy their children's night and try hard not to resent the money that Steve is bringing in, because he works so hard and might or might not make it in time to join us. Again.

At the end of the evening, the children will all parade around the oval and the big girls will take Jack's hand and walk him around for his first lantern parade. The loud speaker will play the Lantern Song in German and I'll try hard not to weep for my first lantern parade in the deep of winter with tiny snowflakes that never made it to the cobbled stones. I'll weep for the girl who believed she owned the world and had worlds to give her own children. I'll weep for the woman who can't make it through a day any more. I'll weep for the old lady who'll wake up one day and find that love was never enough.

Then I'll pack the blanket up, we'll walk back to the car and, after I've tucked them all in bed, I'll dream of what it could be like if only I could remember how to breathe.

*

In A Time Long Ago and A Place Somewhere Else, there was a magnificent castle. In that castle, lived King Steven and Queen Elinor and their three beau-ti-ful children. They were called Princess Bella, Princess Katie, Prince Jack, Queen Mollydog and Baby Elephant…

Queen Elinor was busy in the kitchen setting out mixing bowls and ingredients. She had aprons folded over the backs of chairs and a bowl for each of her children.

Queen Mollydog lay expectantly in front of the fireplace looking excited but trying not to show it. The fireplace had a big basket of pine cones and coloured Christmas balls in it. It was a big basket – actually, a very big basket because it was a very big fireplace. On top of the mantelpiece were a million billion Christmas cards from all over the country and a few beyond that.

Everyone in the castle was singing Christmas carols, not just the Australian ones of summer heat and dust and Santa in rusty utes, but the ones that made you think of cold, cold winters, frosty windows and family. Queen Elinor was humming to herself and occasionally singing a line or two, way off key and with a few unusual words when she forgot how the lines really went.

'That's the wrong note, Ma.' Princess Bella came in, her hat swinging from her arm. 'And the wrong words,' she added.

'Ring the bell please, Bella.' their mother said with a sigh. This could become a very long baking session.

Within a few minutes, there was a thundering of feet as Captain Jack tried racing Baby Elephant to the kitchen. Baby Elephant, who was last, tried skidding to a stop, but he couldn't, so he bowled into Princess Katie, who bowled into her brother and the three of them ended up sliding across the floor and into the fireplace. Well, you can imagine the mess. Pine cones and Christmas balls went flying everywhere. Queen Mollydog, who, if you remember, had been lying in front of the fireplace, moved very quickly but still ended up with the basket upside down on her head.

'Well!' said Queen Elinor. 'That's called An Entrance. Now, everybody wash your hands.' It wasn't until all the children were seated that she noticed Baby Elephant looking very forlorn picking up the pine cones and Christmas balls and putting them back in the basket. 'What's the matter, Baby Elephant?'

'I can't bake, I have no hands!' and he tried to hold up his front feet to show her more clearly.

'Now, that could be a problem,' she agreed, wondering whether he could take her place while she sat down with her feet up for a while. 'Children, how can Baby Elephant do some baking?'

'I think he could use his trunk to stir the mixture round,' Princess Bella suggested.

'Yes,' Princess Katie said and placed the head cook's chef hat on Baby Elephant's head and led him gently over to the table.

He smiled and batted his eyelids at everyone and very carefully wrapped his trunk around the biggest mixing bowl in the kitchen. But once he'd done that, there was no way he could pick up a wooden spoon to start mixing. Everyone could see this was not going to work, so Queen Mollydog, realising that no one had the extra hands, put on an apron (dogs can do this in A Somewhere Else) and held a spoon with her teeth.

The next few hours were happily spent measuring and mixing and baking and sampling. Every now and then, someone or other from around the castle would pop their head in to make sure that the quality of the biscuits was as it should be. Just about everyone was satisfied. The biscuits Queen Mollydog and Baby Elephant made were already packed into special packets to be given as gifts to all the animals on the castle estate as Christmas presents.

But it was in the middle of wrapping all the other baked biscuits and sorting them into their various tins and things that suddenly Captain Jack jumped up and cried out, 'Look! The biscuits are running away!' and sure enough, like a line of ants, little biscuit men and women were jumping out of their boxes, slipping down the table leg and out the door. Lots and lots of them, and some that hadn't even had their clothes painted on yet with icing!

Everybody rushed to the door and there they all were running helter skelter across the courtyard and out into the garden.

'Well, I never!' exclaimed Queen Elinor with her hands on her cheeks making them even dustier with flour than before.

'Look, the hens are chasing them!' Captain Jack laughed, jumping up and down as he pointed to the little biscuits scuttling in all directions. 'Let's chase them too!' and he began running after the little biscuits trying to pick them up and stuff them into his pockets but they kept on jumping out. Some crumbled in his hands and as they landed, I'm afraid, but apart from that, if it was a race, the biscuits were definitely winning.

'Oh dear,' Queen Elinor said, shutting the door to stop any more biscuits running away. 'After all that work.'

They all returned to the table to clean up the baking mess. What they found was Baby Elephant trying to sit on top of the table pressing lids on to the biscuit tins. He had a whole stack of them and all around him were pieces of biscuits that he'd obviously taken bites out of.

'I don't think I want to eat any more gingerbreads or Christmas biscuits.' Princess Katie pulled up her chair to the table and slumped her head into her hands. 'They seemed alive.'

'You know what?' Princess Bella said as she munched on one of the leftovers. 'I don't think they really are alive. Maybe just the men and women biscuits, but I didn't see the kookaburras fly away or the stars float up to the sky or the houses start smoking from their chimneys. Maybe they were just having fun and wanted to play for a day. You have to wonder what biscuits could do all day shut up in their biscuit tins.'

Katie looked at Bella with one of those looks and shook her head. 'I think, Bella, that you've had too much biscuit dough.'

Princess Bella laughed and carried some dishes to the sink, where their mother was washing up. Bella was helping her mother finish putting the lids on the remaining biscuits when King Steven arrived home from work.

'Hello, everyone!' he said with a big smile. All he got in return was a few mumbles and a kiss on the cheek from his wife. 'Well, that's not much of a greeting!' he said, pulling Jack onto his lap and tickling Katie under the arm as he sat down.

'Our biscuits ran away,' Jack said as he tried to climb onto his shoulders. 'And the chickens chased them all over the yard and I tried to catch some and put them in my pocket and Bella ate them.' He said this with an accusing look in Bella's direction.

Baby Elephant quietly wiped a few crumbs from the end of his trunk.

'Well, that sounds exciting.' King Steven smiled at his children. 'They must have had magic flour dust.'

'Yes!' exclaimed Bella, 'I forgot all about that! You remember, Katie,' she turned to her sister with a big wink. 'Tell them about the magic flour dust that the cousins brought back from Kyrgyzstan!'

Princess Katie had scowled at first, when King Steven suggested the flour, but then she thought better of the idea. 'Aaah…' she said, 'the magic flour from Kyrgyzstan where the Mogul kings' horses can fly and the houses are made of gingerbread…'

'And that,' I said, running out of ideas, 'is a story for another time.'

*

I wish I had magic fairy dust.

2 August 2011

To: Bella, Jack

<u>Subject: Dinner's at mine this month</u>

Look how efficient Bella is getting at this!

Poor Mama, I guess she became busier and busier as we all grew older and became involved in so much. You, Jack, seemed to have been dragged from pillar to post. But thank you! It was easier when Bella and I got to high school, because we could just walk to Oma and Opa's until Pa picked us up. But by then you were into sport and stuff. Jack, you must have spent a lot of time in the van.

Anyway, let me know if you're coming,

Hugs and kisses,

Katie plus two

Does Brad count as one or two? :)

3 August 2011

To: Katie, Jack

<u>Subject: No crystal ball</u>

Hello! So close to the end. Probably a good thing we had no crystal ball. We'll be there, Katie. What can I bring?

Love as always

Bella

<u>Attachment:</u>

February 1997

Well, we've got term time down to a fine art now. I've generated a calendar on the computer. Don't you just love computers? I used to laugh at the nerds at school in the computer room and now we all have one in our living rooms. Who'd have guessed how much we'd use them and mobile phones and Nintendos, DVDs – in fact, I bet people won't be using land lines or videos any more in ten years' time. Anyway, this calendar of mine, I printed it out on A3 and each month has the day broken in to seven columns highlighted with a different colour for each member of the family. Each day begins with rules. Each day ends with rules. I wouldn't survive if we didn't keep to this.

Steve drops the girls off at school in Blackwood on his way to work. Bella will be driving in a couple of years, if they don't change the laws. I like to pick them up when I can, though. There's something about that trip home in the car, with the chatter or tears of the day. It all seems to settle by the time we pull into our property and drive up to the house. Funny how everybody's shoulders relax when the car pulls into the garage.

Every morning, Jack and I join Neville in the shed. I love this time with Jack. Next term is kindy. But for now, Jack has his own little workstation, so he's not in the way of all our machinery and mess. He's getting quite good at hammering bits of offcuts together. Sometimes we can even guess what he's made before he tells us!

Neville has employed another chap, Lucas, to help, now and he seems to have the same kind of quirky vision we do. His work is good as well. It also means that Lucas can take on more of the work if Neville cuts back. He's spoken of a retirement plan. Aaaaagggghhh! Maybe then, I could sell the business. Do you think anyone would buy it?

I keep up with the house and cooking by taking bite-size pieces out of the workload. A room a day and Thursday afternoon is shopping; Friday morning, Jack and I cook for the week and pop the meals in the freezer. Oh, freezer, how I love thee!! Once the girls hit secondary school, they had to take on their own washing. This has not solved the 'missing single sock' phenomenon, however. Where do single socks go? Don't tell me.

Everyone's doing well, and growing well. We try and keep Sundays for us, but this is getting harder as they all get older.

March 1998

Hormones! Steve and Bella went toe to toe the other evening – again. She was in a foul mood, rude and snappy. Steve, all male, stood over her and yelled. Let me add, he had tried the voice of reason for two days, but subtle is not one of his strengths. So, poor sausage is grounded this weekend. Unfortunately, this does not improve the mood much.

Boys are so much more energetic, but so much less complicated. So I put another cross on the calendar and wait for another few weeks…

Sigh. Bella threatens to give up the cello, the way the James Bond villains used to threaten to blow up the world.

15th

Good old Jack. Off to kindy with a quick kiss and hug, then a hop, skip and a hurrah. I hated that kindy run; I never really managed to get stuck into anything before the kindy kid had to be picked up. How can children with exactly the same gene pool be so completely different?

Marley and I look really similar and although we chose different studies at uni, she's gifted at music too and I'm sure I could have done law, if I'd wanted to. I wonder if Papa ever wanted a son? Why haven't I thought about that question till now? I never ever doubted he was anything but proud of having two daughters, but there's no one to carry on his business. I guess I've followed a bit in his footsteps, but it's not like taking on the family business. Maybe Jack will; Paddy has followed Simeon into accounting. Michele has gone into business. Jack could be – um – I wouldn't be surprised at anything they all decided to be.

I wonder what partners they'll choose; and what my grandchildren will look like and what their names will be. No crystal ball.

June 1998

I have three children for sale – very cheap, in fact. I'd give them away today! Where's that place that single socks disappear to? There must be an equivalent for at-the-end-of-their-tether mothers, surely. I am so, so tired. Another cold?

23 August 2011
To: Katie, Jack
<u>Subject: The beginning of the end</u>

So here it is. This is where it gets really sad. You might want to take deep breaths. In through the nose and out through your mouth. Like I said earlier, none of this is compulsory reading, I just thought we should at least all have it.

Love as always

Bella

<u>Attachment:</u>

4 April

Yes. Another infection! I just seem to have gone downhill since last term. I came back from delivering some of Red Doors' masterpieces to Sydney. I do love handing them over and watching the clients' faces. I have only had one disappointing reaction so far. Not bad at all.

But I came back with a cold, a sniffle really. So that was four months ago. I seem to go from cold to cold, some a little nastier than others, or like one long sneaky cold that looks like it's gone and then jumps out and yells 'Surprise!' at me, just when I need to be putting more time in to work. I'm so exhausted; it's like being pregnant but different. I've certainly been tired before. Steve's complaining that I'm just overdoing things again and maybe I need to go back to three days a week and let Neville and Tim take over. 'Be a lady of leisure,' is what he said. I think he must have momentarily forgotten the three school-aged children component of our lives! I have to admit, at the back of my head, is a very scary thought.

And another cold! One after another after another. I have this awful dread that this is how I felt last time. Karen has put me on echinacea, and primrose oil and stuff. Anyway, managed to make an appointment for next Wednesday with my old Dr Mac.

15 September 2011
To: Katie, Jack
<u>Subject: Café philosophy</u>

There's a new café in Blackwood. You know, on the Blackwood side of the railway bridge. Fantastic little place called Café de la Paix (Café of Peace). It's a French theme, warm lighting, jazz music down low, very 'ambient'. Anyway, I've started going there before picking the kids up from childcare. Love it.

So I was there the other day and this middle-aged woman stomped in out of the rain. Very businesslike, quick movements – like Mama before she got ill the first time. She looked around the room and chose one of the tables by the windows. Soon afterwards, a young woman walked in, obviously on a lunch break from work and obviously her daughter. They stood up and hugged, really hugged. I was riveted. About five minutes later, another young woman arrived and though she didn't look much like the other two, she clearly belonged with them. Same big hugs. I watched them order, sit down, chat, laugh, scowl and sit in silence. They must have been there for over an hour. I left before they did and as I walked past their window, the mother looked out and smiled. I suddenly felt orphaned. Then I remembered you. Oh, yes, and Pa and Oma and Opa and my own bundles and… Orphaned nevertheless.

Mama left before we got to do much of that sort of thing. She left before we were old enough to have gone our own ways to meet up occasionally for coffee or lunch. Emerge as adults and meet like friends.

We were just starting to get there, but for you younger ones, she was still only your mother. Not *only*! Gosh, I don't mean that was nothing. I mean that our relationships with her hadn't grown old like they have with Pa. We never got to discuss politics much, or get advice on job opportunities. She left us while we were still looking for cuddles and fun and discipline. She left when we could still throw wobblies and know that in five minutes' time we could go back into the sitting room and she'd look at us as if the last time we spoke we hadn't yelled, 'I hate you! You're so unfair!'

I think I was angrier the second time around. I felt like we'd been lied to about the remission. So many almost good years, and because she gave up everything to be there for us, when she got ill again I felt so violated, my trust in adults – her – gone forever. I'm so grateful I managed to fix this. She managed to fix this. She was gutsy that way.

All my love

Bella

<u>Attachment:</u>

29 May 1998

We knew that it wasn't good to be asked to come in together to get my blood test results.

So when Dr Mac himself rang to ask us both to come in, we knew it had to be serious. But I knew, I really knew before the tests, things just weren't right. Again. He sent me back to the oncologist. Again. I sat across the fine desk, every detail suddenly stark and memorable. The photo of a middle-aged woman in a grey silk suit laughing at the younger woman at her side. Obviously his wife and daughter; I found myself admiring the precision of the neatly stacked files on the left of the desk top, my file open with his expensive fountain pen lying askew over the test results. I had a sudden urge to straighten the pen; within seconds, it became almost an obsession. There was also a half-finished cup of coffee in a fine-bone china mug. The pen bothered me. A lot. I looked at the doctor's face and watched his mouth moving, his eyes directed at Steve, darting every now and then to me. I felt Steve reach for my hand and squeeze it. I tried focusing on him, turning my whole body towards him. I squeezed back and shook my head, as if I had water in my ears. It was like I was watching a play looking at all three of us from somewhere else.

'Were there any questions you'd like to ask me?' the doctor asked.

'Yes, can you repeat that again? I think you lost me after "it's not good".'

'It's okay, Elie, I'll fill you in…' Steven began.

'No, tell me again.' I remember taking a sharp breath, so sharp it hurt my throat. 'I want to know everything now. Am I going to die?'

I want my children to be safe. How can I keep them safe if I'm no longer there? Will Steve look after them gently? What can I create for them now that will keep going for them when I am gone? What gift can I give that will keep me present for them? What if they forget what my voice sounds like? What my smile looks like? What the touch of my arms feel like? I'll be nothing any more, just a part of the ether around them. The stars above them. Untouchable, mysterious and invisible. That's how some people see God. How sad to have a god who is untouchable, mysterious and invisible.

They've given me six months to make memories with. I must type out all the stories I can remember and label photographs. I have six months to live. Six months to live all the days of my life.

I want to crawl into bed and wake up tomorrow and not have to go through any of this. I tell the children their stories and make them silly, or special and ending happily. But now, I'm the one with the end and someone else will be picking up the pieces and making the lives of my children happen, be there for their moments of glory and despair. And I, I will only be a part of the music that they play and the dreams they dream, no longer substance in their lives, their little lives.

So who is going to look after me?

Maybe I'll take up music again, maybe the violin. Or maybe I could put all of these stories into a book for the kids for Christmas. Just get the Print Shop to print them in a book; I could even illustrate a few. Ha! That would mean using the computer! I like handwriting them anyway. I think differently when I do that.

*

In A Time Long Ago and A Place Somewhere Else, there was a magnificent castle. In that castle lived King Steven and Queen Elinor and their three beau-ti-ful children. They were called, Princess Bella, Princess Katie, Prince Jack, Queen Mollydog and Baby Elephant…

One morning, the family woke up and decided to go down to the beach. It was a beautiful spring day with promises and kisses of summer all over it. The sky was the same colour blue as it is today.

See how the blue of the sky brightens the colours everywhere? Why is that, do you think? I think it's because we are all together going on a picnic by the sea.

So King Steven ordered the coachman to pack the royal carriage full to the brim of everything the family might need for the whole day.

Baking Day had only just been yesterday so there were lots of baked goodies to take. Let's see: Princess Bella's chocolate-chip cookies, Princess Katie's shortbread, Jack's chocolate cake.

'What did Queen Mollydog bake?' Jack asked with a concerned frown.

'Oh, well, she was a bit like Papa: she was too tired to cook so she just helped to mix and lick the bowl clean afterwards to make sure everything tasted the best it could possibly taste.'

'Oh, that's all right then.'

There were cold pies and ham sandwiches and olives and tomatoes and three kinds of cheeses, and fritz and sauce sandwiches. There were sweet apples from the Magareys' Orchard and sweet nashi pears and bananas and the hugest, sweetest reddest strawberries from Opa's garden.

Princess Bella had gathered all the towels, and bathers and goggles, and snorkels and flippers; Captain Jack had collected as many balls and bats as he could find (it's amazing where you can find balls if you keep looking!); Baby Elephant gathered the hats and lined up everybody's shoes and then spent the next twenty minutes trying them all on and rearranging the order. Princess Katie helped pack the food. Princess Bella was helping her father to manage the packing of the coach.

'I thought the coachman was doing that,' Bella pointed out.

'Well, yes, he was asked, but sometimes King Steven had better ideas of just how that should be done and was very helpfully instructing the coachman.'

'Aah,' Bella said with her twinkly smile; she has such a twinkly smile. 'So, are they ready to go to the beach yet?'

'Yes, Bundle...'

So they were finally ready to go to the beach and they were all sooooo excited. King Steven sat in the middle of one of the enormous seats with his big daddy arms around as many of the children as he could gather. Queen Elinor sat on the opposite side and smiled at her family. She was not very well and so family outings and doing active stuff was quite difficult for her. Sitting in the middle of the bustle and watching helped her feel like she was a part of things still. Baby Elephant had tried hopping onto the front of the carriage where Queen Mollydog and the coachman sat, but it had been kindly suggested that he might have a better view and better exercise if he trotted alongside the carriage.

Princess Katie offered that that might improve his appetite for the picnic and she had specifically packed a case of juicy apples for him to eat all on his own.

'Let's sing songs!' Princess Bella suggested and immediately started one of the never-ending songs that, once you start singing, never ever seem to leave your head. They all joined in with great gusto for ages, maybe even ten minutes before poor Captain Jack put his hands over his ears and started yelling.

What happened next, I'm sad to say, was one of those family arguments where nothing makes sense and everyone has an opinion and no solution. This went on for a very short while until King Steven ordered the coachman to stop the carriage.

'You'll all be walking to the beach if you can't stop this noise! I think it's time your mother told a story.'

The children all blinked at him. Princess Bella looked down the long, long road to the sea and decided to keep quiet. Everyone followed her lead, except Baby Elephant, who thought they were still singing the never-ending song and was trumpeting his own version from somewhere outside. Princess Bella looked out the door to see him swaying contentedly from side to side, swinging his little trunk up in the air. King Steven caught his eye, and Baby Elephant blushed a pretty shade of pink and covered his mouth with his ears.

'Whops, sorry…' he said.

Princess Katie giggled.

'That's all right,' their father said, 'but I think you mean whoops, not whops.'

Baby Elephant looked surprised. 'I do?'

Having delivered this speech, King Steven sat down and gathered everyone back into his arms, kissed the top of their heads and looked over at Queen Elinor, who was starting to feel very tired. She was very tired all the time now, and sometimes telling stories was very difficult because her sleepy brain wouldn't remember the right words to say next.

'Oh, all right, then. Let me see… In A Time Long Ago and a Place Somewhere Else…' and so it began.

The story kept them all happy and quiet until Mollydog started barking excitedly and tapping on the carriage to let them know they were nearly there.

'I can see the sea!' they all cried, because that's what you say when you catch the first glimpse of the sea.

Everyone piled out of the carriage and for once the children were allowed to run off without helping to unpack all their stuff. Queen Elinor watched them all before picking up a basket of towels

'Don't do that,' King Steven said, taking the basket from her. 'Hey, Captain Jack! Come and take the basket for your mother.'

Captain Jack came racing back across the sand to skid to a halt in front of his parents. 'Mama, are your arms too skinny now? I can carry it.' And he carried it away.

King Steven smiled at his son's thoughtfulness. 'I asked Coachman to come so he can help load Baby Elephant up and set out the picnic. Let's just go play.' So hand in hand, they followed the children down to the water.

Halfway down, King Steven had to pick his wife up, which is quite funny because she was the same height as he was. But now she weighed soooo little it was not as difficult as it might have been once.

'Let's build sandcastles!' Princess Bella suggested, and so it began.

The castles would take all day to build and in between construction they would all go off and splash in the water, swimming and playing 'Marco Polo'.

Princess Katie practised cartwheels up and down the beach, but she never quite managed to keep her legs straight so occasionally she would go bottom up in the sand.

Queen Elinor just sat on the beach and counted heads every now and then, or stood by the water distracting Baby Elephant from thinking he could swim.

After a while, it was time to call everyone into the shade for lunch. Everyone had a special towel that fitted over their heads like a cape and dangled all the way down to their knees, even Baby Elephant had one (but – don't tell him I said so – he did look a little bit odd because his bottom and tail never seemed to stay covered properly).

They all ate and ate and ate and ate. They ate until their tummies were so full that Bella thought she was going to bust like a balloon.

'Let's all have a snooze,' King Steven suggested.

Even Captain Jack agreed to this and soon they were all…fast…asleep.

3 November 2011

To: Katie, Jack

<u>Subject: Next bit</u>

Sorry this has taken me so long. I've been avoiding it.

You all know my number and you all know where I live. This is your home too and you can come anytime and sit down on the new trampoline…

Love as always

Bella

<u>Attachment:</u>

3 April

I will not be here for Jack's next birthday.

I can't keep away from my shed, so on good days I go out and fiddle. I feel a bit like Jack must have, me in my little corner so I don't interfere with the real work, or hurt myself.

I'm making a dolls' house. God knows why – I have no little girls left – but this is going to be the dolls' house I never had and the one that every little girl would want.

I will not see the summer. My body can't wait for summer, so today I've brought great branches of autumn into the house and filled the vases with their royal colours. The children are pasting autumn leaves on every scrap of paper. We're making 'curtains' out of them to stick on the sliding doors. I can't see the summer. But Today is beautiful.

Neville is running Red Doors now. I've taken my hands right off. Off and out. I'm glad we planted the pencil pines between my Red Doors shed and the house block. Glad there's a separate entrance from the driveway. Glad that when I can't get down there any more, I won't be able to see clients come and go, or the red truck come and go.

I'm glad the girls are at school. Mollydog follows me around everywhere with her head and tail bowed. She's not feeling great either. She won't even let me go to the loo by myself.

7th

Mutti and I will take Molly to the vet today because she's really worrying me. She's lost her appetite and her back legs are giving her grief. I think her hearing's even worse and I've put it off, because I'm so scared the vet will say she needs to be put down.

The glucosamine isn't working any more. Molldogy and I, we're both deteriorating fast and I wonder which one of us will be the first… I have to go back today to see how my blood tests are. I think, I really think, that I've had enough.

Steven's taking Jack to school now and Bella gets herself and Katie to and from wherever they need to be. Mutti will pick them up. Just until my face isn't grey any more and I can stand upright for more than a minute. I want to be able to watch them play sport after school again.

I'm tired; I'll write again tonight.

May Day 1998

So 'tonight' never happened. Somehow between then and now, weeks have slipped through my cracks. That day, I managed to get Mollydog into an appointment for the next week, and I went to my oncology appointment.

I once carried babies inside my body. I grew and nourished human beings into flesh, muscle, sinew, perfect bodies. Their lives became extensions of ours, bringing life and glory to us. Now, what I am growing in my body has taken me over and it has brought death and decay. I will not recover. We couldn't talk on the way home. Steven just held my hand as he drove.

We took Molly to the vet the following week. She has to be put down and Steven and I think that this would be a good way to start talking about the fact that sometimes we don't get better. Don't you think it's some kind of perverted morality that you can go to jail for keeping animals alive in terrible states, but humans have to go through this devastating process of decay and torture. I wish I was a dog. Or one of the dairy's prize milkers. They'd just take me out the back and kindly shoot me out of my misery.

That last lot of chemo was my last. No more treatment now.

So we've planned a strategy. One of Steven's well-engineered campaigns. We made an appointment for a week away after the vet visit, for 'the' visit. That night, we made a couple of comments around the place noticing how unwell and unhappy Mollydog was looking. A few days later, we wondered whether it was kind to keep giving her medicine just so that we could still have her around, even though it wasn't healing her. We both tried hard not to cry.

Bella and Katie looked at each other straight afterwards and I couldn't meet their eyes for a moment when they looked at me. When I did, that was the moment they understood about Mollydog.

We weren't sure what to say about me. How do you have that conversation with your children? Steve and I both knew that telling them about me would be the hardest part. It was. We put Jack to bed. Then we cuddled up with the girls, on the couch. It was so painful, but Steven did the talking and explained it and let them ask questions and when the terrible, terrible truth of my prognosis settled in their eyes, we all broke down and sobbed together.

We asked them not to go telling everyone just yet, to maybe just choose a couple of really special people. We agreed to tell Jack the next day. We would all take the day off and spend it together. I hate to do this to them in the middle of the school year. Dear God, one who I'm trusting is present, knowable and seen, I know there,s no purpose in the question 'Why?' So I'm pleading that this will be the ground of strength and family-ness and deep, deep capacity to love even though it's risky. May this be the lesson they all learn.

The dolls' house is looking good.

I can't sleep again tonight. I lie awake and will my bones to rest. This constant aching is breaking me down. I feel like my body's a battleground and the soul of me is being trampled and ripped apart. How violated and ravaged the fields and forests of Europe must have felt while centuries of armies ripped the earth and composted blood into the soil.

I lay awake for ages and watched Steve's profile, I even reached out and traced his silhouette with my finger. He's going to need his sleep over the next few weeks, months. Oh God! I'm going to be lying here in this bed being eaten away slowly; eaten until I can no longer stay in my home and then I'll lie in a hospital bed and start to smell of death. I'll watch their little faces, my precious faces, try not to feel bad about not wanting to come close, or touch me. I understand why some would choose to avoid that. I want to slit a hole in my back and pull my backbone out. Just so that I can sleep. I don't have to need it out permanently, just give me six hours. Even four. I'd settle for one if I could sleep deeply. And when the sun rises and the children wake up one by one, they'll jump into our bed or call out from the kitchen and I'll go in and make porridge or toast.

And when they're all gone, I'll crawl back into bed and pray for oblivion.

Listen to that wind. The rustle of dry gums as the branches sway in the night breezes.

I love that sound. I used to love that sound. Now it sounds a little mournful and I wonder whether sounds I love will remind the children of me. Will they think about me in catches of memory? Will they hold their breath through the train tunnels? Will they still dance in the rain and lick the baking bowl? Who will watch them become parents as a mother watches? I hate that person. Whoever she is, I hate her. I hate her because it won't be me. I'll never watch them hold their own children in their arms, watch their tummies swell with pregnancy, watch them create traditions of their own. I wish I could have been more than I was, more than I am.

I want to wake him and make him hold me, hold me and tell me it'll all be all right, that I'm still beautiful and the desire of his eyes. That if I close my eyes he'll hold me until the pain goes away again.

Instead I just lie here and type on my laptop. Tomorrow is not another day. No more tomorrows, just one interminable long nightmare day of sun and moon and eating away of life. My life. Our life.

We took a picnic up to Mt Lofty Botanical Gardens today. It has to be the most stunning place in autumn; it never ceases to delight and invigorate me with the glorious richness of colour and texture. We kicked our way through mounds of crackly brown leaves and still-moist golden, red and yellow leaves. Jack managed to climb his favourite tree and Bella actually joined him, which was hysterical, because she's so tall now. Mollydog came too and we brought a warm rug for her to lie on while we sat at the picnic table. I began this last story on the drive home.

'The time has come, the Walrus said…'and so it has. I'm not going to write again after this. This will take me a while to write, so:

My Bundles.

I love you with my last breaths and I will go on loving you when I am only breath.

Love well, laugh often and live all the days of your lives.

*

In A Time Long Ago and A Place Somewhere Else, the family were all enjoying the summer holidays.

'You've forgotten the beginning, Mama.' Jack sat up suddenly.

'Pardon?'

'The beginning – there was a magnificent castle…'

'Oh yes.'

There was a magnificent castle. In that castle lived King Steven and Queen Elinor and their three beau-ti-ful children. They were called Princess Bella, Princess Katie, Prince Jack, Queen Mollydog and Baby Elephant…

The family were all enjoying the summer holidays.

'But it's winter now!' Jack corrected again as he stroked Bella's scarf.

'Well, yes. But it wasn't now. Can it still be the summer holidays?'

He sighed, shrugged. 'Nyeh, I don't mind.'

'I suppose it doesn't really matter. It can be winter holidays.'

Okay, so the family decided to go on a holiday. A long, long holiday. A holiday so long it needed toothbrushes and shampoo to be included in the packing. They were all going to go to the snow! Queen Elinor hadn't been to the snow since she was a teenager in an even further away land and the children had never been to the snow at all. Baby Elephant and Queen Mollydog had never seen the snow either. Baby Elephant didn't even know what snow was, but he didn't want to appear ignorant so he swayed his trunk and smiled and said all the right things, like 'How nice!

How exciting! The snow, hey? Fancy that!' Queen Mollydog wagged her tail twice and then put her head back down on her front paws.

Everyone began to hustle and bustle about writing lists and going through their wardrobes to dig out their bathers and their flippers.

'Hang on, a minute, Mama. Didn't you say that they were enjoying the summer? But now they're going to the snow?' Katie interrupted me.

'Oh, whoops! I suppose it would be a bit cold for bathers, but maybe they were going somewhere that had a spa! Like Oma and Opa's spa, with lots of luscious warm bubbles in a hot tub in a room that makes you feel like you are staying on a tropical island. They have those sometimes at snowing holidays.'

Katie sighed. 'Okay, that would work. But no flippers. I thought you were just getting confused again.'

Bella nudged her in the ribs and everyone else just looked embarrassed.

'What do you mean again? I don't get confused very often…'

Steve's face was pink and he just kept driving.

Katie looked me in the face, smiled brightly and carried on, 'So, they put all their spa gear in one spot and began writing more lists for the winter clothing. They were going to do heaps of really fun things, like learn how to make a snowman from real snow and…' She paused and looked at me.

I blinked and said, 'That's right, they were going to build the best and biggest and the friendliest snowman in the whole history of A Place Somewhere Else.'

They were also going to learn how to ski downhill. Captain Jack was going to do it without skis, and Princess Katie was going to learn figure skating and become a world champion at it in nanoseconds; and King Steven was going to try his hand at ski jumping and Princess Bella was going to race King Steven in tobogganing.

Baby Elephant was feeling a bit left out, so he waited for a quiet moment before approaching their mother. 'I hope you don't mind me asking, but exactly what are elephants good at in the snow?'

'Oh, well – that's a surprise, Baby Elephant, an exciting, let's-wait-and-see surprise.'

'Really? A surprise?' A small frown appeared between his lovely blue eyes. 'Do you mean like a birthday surprise? Or more like a Jack-is-about-to-leap-out-from-on-top-of-a-cupboard-on-top-of-you surprise?'

'A special birthday surprise.'

Baby Elephant seemed happy at that and went to collect as many boxes, suitcases, coats and paraphernalia that needed fetching, carrying or moving.

Queen Mollydog was feeling really tired that day and her poor old legs were hurting her quite a lot. The children's happy chatter was like music to her, but, you know what, she just couldn't join in the packing, so Baby Elephant ran around and did the little Queen Mollydog bits that she would normally have done. He didn't mind; he knew she wasn't well enough any more.

'What's wrong with Queen Mollydog? Is she really ill?' Jack asked, his fingers drawing greasy patterns all over the car window.

'I'm afraid so, Jack. It happens that way sometimes. In fact, with everything living. Sometimes we live long and healthily, or it can sometimes be short and not very well at all. Queen Mollydog was not so old, but very sick. Our Mollydog is very old and very sick too.'

'That's sad,' Katie said, her eyes looking suddenly very big, as she started to understand where my story was heading.

'Shall I go on? They're about to have a fabulous holiday.'

There was silence in the back seat.

Okay, so everybody was packing up ready for their long drive to the snow. It was going to take all night and all day to drive there, so King Steven had the coachman pack the carriage up the night before, ready to harness the horses when they were ready to leave in the middle of the night. It was going to be an exciting adventure and it would begin in the dark. They would drive for hours until breakfast and keep driving east until they finally reached the snowfields, way, way up in the Eastern Mountains.

All the children decided to sleep together in front of the big fireplace, snuggled up together on the couches and chairs, because that was the best way to start new adventures.

Sometime in the middle of the night, King Steven and Baby Elephant carried the sleeping children – even the big princesses, Bella and Katie – to the carriage. There were a few toilet stops first – just in case. It wasn't long before everyone was bundled up under warm quilts and feather pillows with water bottles and snuggle bears clasped in their arms. They were off! Coachman had harnessed the horses and the jangle of their bits and the clop of their feet on the cobblestones was soothing, and the gentle rock of the carriage soon had them all nodding back off to sleep.

They travelled for hours under the clear night skies, hours and hours through the dark corners of the countryside. The air was so crisp and clear that Queen Elinor thought, as she looked out of the window, that if she just reached up her arms, she'd be able to gather a whole bunch of stars and draw them into the carriage for her children.

Princess Katie was the first one to wake up. The sun had not yet risen on the cold winter morning and she'd woken up with her usual bounce and energy.

'Just look at the stars, Katie. Don't they look so close?'

Princess Katie moved over and tucked herself under her mother's arm.

They sat there for a while, until Queen Elinor said, 'One day, if ever we're not together, and you're feeling very alone, you just have to look up into the sky. The stars that are shining on you, they'll be shining on me too and I'll be loving you. They'll be my kiss goodnight and your sleeping will be my cuddles.'

Katie looked up at her mother, nodded and smiled.

Soon everybody was awake and demanding breakfast. Captain Jack began looking for ways to climb up the upholstery in the carriage, but it was a bit difficult with his seatbelt, all the quilts, pillows and sisters in the way. They stopped at the very next highway inn. Coachman took the horses away to have a rest and a feed, and King Steven took his family to have a run around and some breakfast. Baby Elephant picked Queen Molly up in his trunk and carried her carefully into the inn. I think I should mention here that because they were the royal family everybody who knew them understood that they had a baby elephant who was like one of the family, and that Molly the dog was a very famous and beloved citizen of the land. So it was perfectly acceptable for them both to be allowed into a restaurant.

Everybody was happy to be sitting at the table waiting for the enormous breakfast. It was a family favourite of crispy bacon and eggs, eggs fried, poached, scrambled, mushrooms sautéed (that's a special way of frying) in butter, lemon and herbs, tomatoes, freshly baked bread rolls, cheese, croissants, jams, and fruit. Such a feast! And it was only breakfast! Queen Elinor sat beside Queen Molly and helped her to eat, but Queen Molly just wagged her tail. This was going to be a difficult holiday for her, but she wanted to be with her family, so was happy to come.

Soon they were on their way again, swaying in the carriage and singing outrageous and silly songs that never ended. Molly howled tunelessly, in her own special way, Baby Elephant whistled and everybody else sang at the top of their voices.

The Coachman put cotton wool in the horses' ears and earmuffs over his, so that they wouldn't get distracted from the driving. At least, that's why he said he covered their ears, but I think, perhaps, if you could have heard them all, you might have wanted to block your ears too!

Hours passed. They played cards, Queen Elinor read stories, they had little naps, a picnic lunch in some scrub, and just as Captain Jack was wondering for perhaps the hundredth time – out loud – whether they were there yet, and Princess Katie had finished her fifth novel, Coachman knocked politely on the window into the carriage.

'See those lights, your Highnesses. That's the snowfields.'

They'd all been so busy squirming inside the world of the carriage that they'd forgotten to keep an eye on the changing scenery and when they looked out, they could see in the fading light of the winter's day that there were patches of snow everywhere, over the paddocks and beside the road. In the short distance away, they could see snow-covered mountains and the twinkly welcoming lights of Snowfield Town.

Queen Elinor looked over at King Steven and whispered, 'This is going to be such a good holiday. I just hope that Molly will manage it.'

Molly wagged her tail and looked happily around at her favourite people.

The castle they stayed in was smaller than their magnificent castle at home. But there was everything you could want in a winter palace. It was made of shining ice, but inside it was magically warm and cosy and dry. It was full of reflected light from all the icicles, so there was no need for lots and lots of electricity. There were even fireplaces that cast wonderful flickers of warm red light and heat into the room and the ice never melted!

'Ah, Mama…you know that's not actually possible, right? The, um, the heat would melt the ice.' Bella explained this quietly to me.

'I know, Bundle, but doesn't it sound fantastic? Wouldn't it be amazing to stay in a really truly ice palace that was also warm and snugly?'

All the children suddenly felt wide awake and ready for action. They each carried their suitcases into the palace and up the circular staircase to the bedrooms. These were amazing and each child had their own room which interlinked with a series of ice rollercoasters and slippery dips and fireman's poles. The beds were huge and had big fluffy quilts and pillows already made up and looked very inviting. The children's bedrooms were laid out in a triangle shape. The space in the middle could be reached by a door from each room and was an enormous bathroom with a big, warm bubbly spa bath. This, of course, was covered and could only be opened by a grown-up.

After they'd all unpacked their bags, the children all went downstairs to find their parents. They were sitting on a couch together in front of an enormous fireplace. There were plenty of cosy cushions, and chairs and couches for everyone and even Baby Elephant and Queen Molly had somewhere special to sit. Queen Molly was actually feeling quite well for a change, sat up and wagged her tail at them all.

'What's for dinner, Mama?' Princess Katie asked.

'Let's go and see,' and you should have seen what there was!

There was freshly made tomato soup with crusty bread and cheese, then there was a really chunky full-of-fresh-vegetables-and-beef stew with more warm bread rolls, and for dessert there were all kinds of warm puddings and icebcream or cream. The children were suddenly ravenous, so they jumped up to the table and grabbed each other's hands ready to say grace.

That evening they played games and drank hot chocolate until it was time for bed. They all went upstairs and jumped into their warm fluffy beds and snuggled down for their first night in the Ice Castle.

By the time everyone had come down for breakfast the next morning, the winter sun had begun to make itself seen through the windows. They discussed the morning's plans: they were all going to have ice skating lessons in the morning and skiing lessons in the afternoon.

'But first,' their father said, 'we're going to build the biggest snowman ever!'

Everyone was really excited about this and scrambled through brushing their teeth and hair and pulling on all the layers of warm and waterproof clothing to go out into the snow.

Captain Jack was the first out the front of the palace. He'd got ready so fast that while he was waiting for everyone he thought he'd gather a pocket full of snow grenades and hide behind a statue to throw them at everyone. He'd gathered quite a lot before he realised that, actually, snow close to the body melts, and he had to change quickly to Plan B, which was to hide behind the corner of a wall and gather a pile of snowballs on the ground.

The first one out was Princess Bella. The first snowball collected her in the knees. She quickly dashed behind another wall opposite her brother and the fight was on! Unfortunately, everyone else chose to walk out of the doors at that point and running and tumbling across the entrance to the castle, they were torpedoed with snowballs everywhere! Very quickly, the game became Captain Jack and Princess Bella against everyone else. I'm embarrassed to say that Jack and Bella won. In the middle of the battlefield was a great pile of smashed snowballs of all sizes. This they soon turned into the first ball of their winter snowman. Building a snowman was actually quite hard work and it took several of them all to roll the snowballs together. In the end, they had to get several of the palace guards to help them put the snowman together. Now to decorate it! Off they scampered in different directions and in no time there was a pile of pine cones, twigs…

I'm too tired now, kids. Do you mind if I finish this later?

No one said they minded. I minded. Not even Katie finished it off.

9 May 1997

Mollydog died today. We all went in to the vet. Steven carried her and the vet very kindly let Jack hold her while he put the needle in. The vet looked like he wanted to cry too. We were shameless and there aren't enough tissues in the world to stop the tears.

We buried her under the pine tree by the trampoline. The kids slept the night in sleeping bags there, Jack in between the girls. Bella wrapped him in her arms. What will they do when I go? Will they spend nights outside on the trampoline still? Will they hold each other and whisper their secrets into the clear night air until sleep comes to hold them all? So many questions that I can't see the answer to.

28 November 2011

To: Bella, Jack

<u>Subject: Dolls' House</u>

You know, I'd forgotten about the Doll's House. I wonder where it went? Have you looked in the shed, Bella? It would be good to see it again.

Katie xoxo

PS: Can I have it if you do find it?

PPS: I bet Mollydog was pleased to see her.

29 November 2011

To: Bella, Katie

<u>Subject: Molly</u>

I can't believe that's all she wrote about Mollydog! There isn't a memory I have of my childhood that Mollydog wasn't a part of. When she died, before Mama got really sick, we buried her under the pines and that was the first time I saw Pa cry. How did you not even mention this? Neville made the coffin and Pa and I carried it to the grave. I asked Pa how long it was between her death and Mama's. I didn't realise it was so close.

Neville made Mama's coffin too, didn't he?

J

2 December 2011

To: Katie, Jack

<u>Subject: I'd forgotten that…</u>

Yes, Jack, Neville did make her coffin. I'd forgotten that. When it came to Mama, he kept shaking his head, but he made such a lovely coffin and painted it red.

I agree, Katie, it's been a long year. Nearly there. Her birthday was last week. I enjoyed your phone calls, thank you. It was nice going around to Opa and Oma's for tea. Little Noah was, of course, the healing focus. Katie, Mama would have taken him on her lap, and gathered my two in and let them all help her blow the candle out. Some things are just not right.

I rang Pa to ask him about the doll's house. He didn't know, so I rang Opa. Opa told me that Mama gave it to him to finish, but he's never been able to. I wonder if he would if we asked him…

BTW, Jack, of course partners are welcome for family tea. Finally!

Sorry, Jack, I nearly forgot to answer you! Mama died only about four weeks after Molly, and Opa built a bench under the pine tree where Molly was buried so that we could sit and look over the gully… Mama wasn't really conscious during the last week. The end was surprisingly quick. I guess that was good for everyone.

Sitting at my table here, it's midnight and my children are both tucked up in bed. Lachie and I have given them hugs and kisses from all their aunties and uncles and we've prayed for all of their loved ones. I watched the light fade through their window and onto their beds and remembered our bedroom in the Little House, when we girls shared and she would come and tuck us in and read us stories and sing us lullabies and say prayers. Then I remembered how when we moved to the Big House, we'd all still climb into each other's beds or all crash on the family room floor together. We're more than just our DNA, we're beings hardwired to our tribe, to receive and give love. We belong somehow. From the tiny creatures my children are, to the old, old bodies of our grandparents, we're hardwired for relationship. We have voracious (great word) appetites for connection. This is what separates us from our experience, and tells us that the pain and the effort really is worth the while.

Beyond the realms of my own grief lies the truth of our lives. What is true about us in the created sense, and what is true about us in an experiential sense, and what possibilities, as yet unknown, are true about us in the future: this is what loving and being loved explores and sounds out for us. Sounds out like the underwater echoes of sentient mammals that, although unheard, reverberate throughout an unseen world until they find an object to bounce off and be received by and sent back, giving a sense of how deep and wide our space is and what shape it takes. But even deeper, more profound than that, it speaks back about the other, giving us a sense of how deep and wide their space is too.

Am I getting too carried away? Sorry, it's the teacher in me. No comments from you, Katie.

Anyway, I'm trying to summon up some Christmas spirit in my young children. I've put Peter Combe on the sound system on repeat.

This year has been exhausting. I suddenly miss Mama more this Christmas than I have since the first one after she died.

Lachie and I took Madi and Jack to the pageant again last week. Of course it was hot. But we'd found a spot early and had a picnic breakfast just at the beginning, so we didn't have so long to wait for the whole parade to go past.

Anyway, I had a memory of Mama and Pa taking us there. Jack was little. After, we went down to Rundle Mall to see the John Martin's Christmas displays. We were 'oohing and ahhing' over the bright displays of various scenes, when I was elbowed by a woman to my left. She was beside a younger woman holding a child about four years old.

'Ooops, sorry!' the lady began automatically.

Mama just guided me around to the other side of her body. She was so tall and present, wasn't she? Hiding behind her was easy and safe. I turned back to admire the windows and Katie was busy squinting up into the tops of the displays to see how the lights worked.

'I do love the window displays,' the younger woman said to the other. 'They're so bright and pretty.'

'Yes.' The older one placed a hand on the window. 'Your grandmother used to bring us down here every Christmas to see these. It was a special occasion. We'd all be dressed up and then she'd take us to the Balfour's Café for frog cakes.'

The first woman laughed and turned her head. 'Why would you dress up?'

'Going to the city was a special thing. We always dressed up. Which window do you like the best?'

Mama had been asking us the same question in about the same tone of voice. So it was kind of funny.

'Well, would you look at that!' the younger woman suddenly said, as if she was spitting out something sour.

I turned quickly to see which window she was looking at. It was of the nativity. It was beautiful. There was a soft warm light; the adoring figures around the manger were about two feet high. The expressions on Mary's and Joseph's faces were so realistic – tender and reverent. I couldn't see the offence in the display at all.

'These are supposed to be Christmas decorations! Bloody Christians – trying to bring Jesus into everything!'

Mama just laughed out loud. 'Christ – Christ-mas,' she said to the woman. 'No Christ, then no Christmas traditions. I think you've lost the meaning.'

I was so embarrassed. Mama just took our hands and walked us away towards the station.

Losing the meaning of things, that was one of the things that used to annoy her. Traditions, little rituals. The ritual, the pattern, the cadence of family. 'Why? Just because it's important!' she'd say. If we wanted to know why we had to go to some party, or birthday, or opening, she'd say, 'It means something.' So we went. When she was gone, we were able to keep going because the little patterns were there and those little patterns we repeat in our own lives and in our children's lives. Little moments become part of a bigger picture.

And so she's gone. But we're still here. Not those children any more. We were angry, sad, lost and found. We became resilient and bounced back, but we were never the same. We all had to go through the first Christmas without her, our first birthdays, her birthday, school and sporting achievements, illnesses, weddings, births – all without her. Where she should have been. But she wasn't.

Gradually we began to say it didn't matter, even though it did. The weddings and the birth of our children, she should have been a part of, and those are the aching moments. But, life has gone on, we are not crippled, or deprived. We are still who we are largely because of who we all were when she was here. Our family shaped us that way. Our family shape changed and so did we. But I think we can all say that – mostly – we have all lived the days of our lives.

Don't forget, we all have to work out Kris Kringle this week. And who's bringing what for Christmas dinner? Pa's going to provide the drinks. Are you all coming? Anyway, I've attached a reminder invitation for Twelfth Night.

Yours as always,

Bella

You Are Invited to 'Whispers on the Trampoline'
Where: The Big House
When: This Twelfth Night, 9 p.m.
Why: To Remember
What to bring: Your self, your whole self and nothing but yourself

6 January 2013

To: Bella, Jack

<u>Subject: A new story</u>

This started as a story. I wanted to tell it like Mama used to. But I couldn't finish it that way. Writing in the third person about this wasn't possible. So it changes. I could change it. But I'm not going to. I promised to send you both a copy.

'So,' as Mama would say, here it is. 'In all its warts.'

I love you both sooo much.

Katie

Xoxox

<u>Attachment:</u>

In a time not so long ago and a place closer than one of Mama's hugs is a Big House. It stands on the crest of a hill, facing the setting sun and surrounded by bush. In the back garden on the side of the house is a magnificent, but young, oak tree just seventeen summers old. And under that oak tree is a trampoline.

Under that tree, for many years, there sat a table and six wooden chairs that replaced another, far older, far less spectacular trampoline, but now, all is as it should be. The table and chairs sit under a new garden house nearby.

One warm summer Twelfth Night, three grown-ups took their chairs out of the garden house and sat around this new trampoline while two little people jumped and squealed and squabbled and finally fell asleep. Their father came and carried them off to bed one by one.

This was not just any night. This was the Twelfth Night; the night when Christmas decorations are carefully taken down and boxed for another year, a night when the Three Wise Men are said to have arrived to worship the Christ Child in his manger. A night for gifts.

These three grown-ups used to play on their trampoline in this exact same spot when they were just children, but tonight they were older and two of them had children of their own and their hearts were overwhelmed by memories of a Time Long Ago when life had to change. It grew heavy under the strain of it until it broke and took on a new and sometimes scary shape. Their mother died.

But that's not where the story ends. This story, like all good stories, begins with her invitation for them to live all the days of their lives. To live even when she couldn't be there any more. To make sure this happened, she left thousands of stories, and memories and family traditions and a little brown suitcase filled with the memories that she loved and wanted to keep alive for herself.

So this night, this Twelfth Night, the three grown-ups sat around their mother's little brown suitcase and began remembering. Each little item came out one by one: keys to her father's toolbox wrapped around in a softened-by-age leather wallet, love letters that each of her children wrote her for birthdays and Mother's Days and for no reason at all. Photographs, the old-fashioned kind that came in envelopes with a little pocket to hold all the negatives, which the oldest sister had ad copied for all of them. A scrapbook filled with the story of her own little furniture business with the bright Red Door; the story of how it grew and grew like their family and the little oak tree she planted from an acorn she grew in a tub by her back door, underneath some herbs, until it shot through the earth. She picked the acorn up from a really big oak tree that draped its long heavy branches down to the ground and in summer would be clothed in green to make a leafy room. The tree made a room just perfect to weave magical stories around until it became a castle in a place far away and a time long ago. The little acorn grew in that pot by the back door of the little house until it, like the family, grew too big and became ready to be planted in their new house. Oak tree, children, Red Door and all.

She wrote about her children; she wrote stories about the chickens they had, their own garden patches, the games they played. She wrote it all down in bits and pieces.

The eldest sibling had been scanning their mother's diary over the year. She had begun by talking about the last time they'd all gathered together, not long after their mother had died. How they'd all, as children, climbed onto the little old trampoline to talk. They'd begun by talking about the memories of their mother that were still fresh in their very sad hearts. One of them had said that they were scared they'd forget her, the sound of her voice, or the way she talked. And over the years, they did forget. Oh, not the memory of her, but her self. The diaries had brought her back in some way; touched on emotions they had placed in their own boxes somewhere in their minds. This night it was time to take them out, and blow them off into the summer night like dust from a bookshelf.

'Jack, here are a few photos of you and Mama in the shed!' the eldest said, lifting some photos out and placing them in front of her brother. 'And here's that copper ring you made her!'

The ring was a bit green, but held inside a little box with a piece of scrap paper and scrawled across it in their mother's small intense handwriting: 'From my Jack. Captain Jack brought this back from the dragon's lair just for me. He sailed the seas and climbed a mountain, fought a dragon and stole all his treasure. On the way home, he told me, a great swirling surrounded his ship and a sea monster the size of the State Bank rose up and tried to steal the treasure. Captain Jack just escaped with the most precious jewel of all, this ring, which he gave to me. I am deeply honoured.'

Jack, with all that imagination, why did you choose accounting? What part of you closed that door when she died? You sat in the Tree House for weeks, just you and your captain's chest. You climbed down one day and never went back again. I think that if she were here, she'd climb up and get you, she'd wrap you in her strong arms and hold you until you stopped fighting, and then she'd hug you and whisper into your hair. Her breath would be warm against your hair and ear, and she'd tell you how much you're loved; how much Molly had loved you, how much she and Papa love you and how I love you and how the whole world was waiting for this young lad to become an extraordinary young man and fill the whole world with his laughter, creativity and energy.

She'd climb down the ladder and hold her arms out and you'd close your eyes and jump into them. She was so strong, she'd catch you and spin you around until your feet touched the ground and then she'd walk back to the house with her slow, steady tread and you'd scamper off to a brand new adventure. I think you can be safe again now, Jack. Is this why you went from job to job, restless and uninspired? Is this why you've gone back to woodwork again? I think you should go out and slay some dragons!

Bella, you and I should have taken this the best, but maybe we didn't. You and Oma divided the chores for a while and then you took over. You always looked so resilient. You were so confident that it would all be fine. So silent about her growing weakness. You and I would sit up with her sometimes, when Pa was away and Jack was in bed. We would sit and listen to her Chopin CDs, doing our homework. She would doze and occasionally, you'd ask her a question and she'd try and answer it, and sometimes she'd get a bit confused and I'd say something rude. You'd just shrug and laugh, saying, 'Ah, that's where I get it from. Mama, you could have given me your musical abilities instead.' Which she did. Maybe the gift that your grieving gave us all was that you refused to give in to the tragedy, almost like you refused to believe in it; and that meant you could keep us going in our grief.

The only time you broke down was in that last two weeks and everyone was trying so hard and I threw a wobbly. I shouted and ranted and raved about how unfair it all was and how stupid everybody was trying to play happy families when it was all broken, our whole family was broken. I'd given up using glass and crockery because I thought that, if I could go for an entire week without breaking anything, Mama would get better. It all fell apart for me when I broke her grandmother's porcelain candlestick. That was when I knew she was going to die.

Oma started crying, Jack ran up the Tree House and Papa shouted back at me and Mama let her tears run down. She didn't weep, just let the tears run down her face. I felt so ashamed and you wouldn't speak to me for a week. Such a week! I was too proud and too angry to apologise to everyone. Especially not to Mama.

A few days later – it was almost the end – she asked Oma to send me into her room with her drink. So Papa was sitting in the window seat in their room at his table and Oma followed me in. I put the drink by her bed and she held out her hand. Her skin was like paper over her wide fingers, and in her hand was the candlestick.

Had Mama fallen to pieces? No, there it was glued back together from how many pieces? Look at all that gold paint to cover up the glue!

Do you remember she kept it by her bed with her – even in hospital.

She told me it was her 'Chawan', her Japanese tea bowl, where the imperfections are so greatly prized that they're sometimes covered in gold and face the front for all the world to see. She then pored her tea into it and drank.

'Katie,' she said, 'it makes perfect sense that you're angry. It's right to be angry about injustice. It isn't fair for me to leave you like this. And if I could change this, you know I would. But I know you love me and I know you know I love you. There's nothing more to be said.'

I think if she had got cross with me, or begged me to apologise, I would have crossed a line and never come back. But she gave me space to get it all wrong, make a mess of my goodbyes and still know I was loved. If she hadn't, I might not have been there with you at the end.

'So', as Mama would say, we're still five of us, no more, no less, and we've branched off like the oak tree. Some of us now have little ones of our own and new castles to build. But at the core of us, we know that this is where it all began.

7 January 2013

To Katie, Jack

<u>Subject: A quieter year</u>

Oh, wow! That was the best beginning to a New Year I have ever had. Jack – you legend – you made it! Thank you to whatever her name is who pulled all those strings for you to get here. BTW what IS her name…? :)

So how about an annual thing? Same bat time, same bat channel, next Twelfth Night?

I'm going to go into withdrawal now that there's no more diary to scan and no box left to sit over.

Thank you for letting me keep the suitcase. It's sitting in the corner of my study and has my copy of her diary in it. The real diary has its best home with Katie, who's going to turn it into a book. Aren't you, Katie. Note there's no question mark there!

Jack, what did you think of Katie's story? I loved it. Juuust perfect. Thank you. But thank you more than anything for the dolls' houses. You completed Mama's and made two more. You turned them all into castles and I love the red doors at their entrances. Perfect. Anyway, that's it from me. Who's coming to Pa's birthday? Family tea is as always the first Friday of the month. Just let me know.

All my dearest and best to all my dearest and best,

Bella xoxoxoxo